VIRGILANTE

To Jess,

thankyou for Supporting
my writing.
Hope you enjoy the Story!

Joe

JOE EARDLEY

26.01.2021

For Pippa and Bonnie, who love stories

Other books by Joe Eardley:

Powder

Coming 2021:

You Can't Choke an Owl

For an up-to-date list of Joe Eardley's other books, visit

his Facebook page:

https://www.facebook.com/joeeardleybooks/

You can follow him on Instagram:

@joe_eardley_books

'Do I not destroy my enemies when I make them my friends?'

Abraham Lincoln

TABLE OF CONTENTS

CHAPTER ONE

THE HUMILIATION OF ZELDA MCALLISTER

'*I'm going to ask them to move.*'

'*Virgil! What are you doing? Close that door now!*'

'*No, Mum, I'm going to ask those lads to move.*'

'*Virgil, no! Get back in the car this instant! Virgil!*'

Virgil McAllister had a sense of Déjà vu, but this time, he was really going to do it. Every Saturday, they would drive around Asda car park looking for a disabled spot, and every Saturday, not a single space remained. There were sports cars and work vans, motorcycles and SUVs, each one taking up a precious slice of parking real-estate. But nowhere for Zelda McAllister to park her car.

It wasn't as though Virgil believed every space-taker to be illegitimate. He absolutely understood that you could drive an Aston Martin DB11 and be disabled. He also knew, based on his experience of trips out with his grandfather, that you could be a skilled physical labourer and still need a blue badge. Gramps used to have a special pouch on the windscreen of his plasterer's van.

What Virgil struggled to understand was the people who could walk just fine, who would swing into a handicapped bay in their Zafira, leaving four kids strapped in the back while they nipped into the store for some Malibu and a copy of TV Choice. He had felt the injustice of these moments long before his mother became a wheelchair user, but now that she was, Virgil came face-to-face with the issue on a regular basis. But he was only fifteen, what could he do about it?

'Ho-hum, another day, another chocka car park,' Zelda McAllister span the wheel of her hand-controlled Corsa as she circled the store for the third time.

'It's not full though is it, Mum?' said Virgil. 'There are plenty of spaces for regular people to get parked.'

'You saying I'm not a regular person?' Zelda looked sideways at her son, her eyes crinkling.

'Go shops!' squealed Maisie from her car seat.

'You know what I mean,' Virgil drummed on his knees as they passed the heaving parent and child bays.

'I do,' said Zelda, 'but sometimes, the good Lord makes life slower so we can appreciate it better.' Virgil puffed up his cheeks in frustration. He hated it when his mum was gracious in the face of adversity. *How can the good Lord be good after what he let happen to you?*

Oldley Asda's car park was split in two: a sprawling area at the front with around fifteen disabled spots, and a sheltered area to the side with another six. They plunged into the semi-darkness, where thick concrete pillars held up an oppressively low ceiling. Virgil always felt uncomfortable here, away from the bright green shopfront with its flower baskets and charity workers. Zelda indicated left and they crawled past the disabled spaces again, desperately looking for a gap. Still nothing.

In the last blue badge space—the one closest to the supermarket entrance—there sat a souped-up Citroen Saxo. It was cobalt blue and had been parked at an angle— half in the shade, half out. Three young men were outside the car smoking. Two of them sat on the bonnet with their shirts off, introducing their pasty chests to the sun for what looked like the first time that Summer. *It's nearly July, have these guys been using factor fifty?*

'Oh well,' said Zelda, beginning to drive away. 'Shall we try Tesco instead?'

'No, Mum! You shouldn't have to. Look at those lads. Pull up by a parking attendant and ask him to make them shift.'

'Nah, we don't want any trouble. Not with Maisie here too. People entitled enough to park there are never reasonable. Come on, let's go.'

Virgil opened his door.

'I'm going to ask them to move.'

'Virgil! What are you doing? Close that door now!'

'No, Mum, I'm going to ask those lads to move.'

'Virgil, no! Get back in the car this instant! Virgil!'

He slammed the door, pacing away from his mother's frantic shouts. Adrenaline pounded a deafening rhythm in his ears, drowning out all the ambient noise. His hearing returned, pin-sharp, as he stopped abruptly beside the Saxo.

The shortest of the three lads was facing him, he had close-cropped black hair and looked like a discount Michael Peña. He was busy lighting a spliff and hadn't seen Virgil yet. *Oh, crud.* There was a fourth lad in the driver's seat. Virgil could only see a left arm, but his tattoo sleeve had enough skulls on it to confirm that this was a bad idea. *Too late now.* They had noticed him. Michael

Peña took a long drag, narrowing his eyes, then alerted the other two. They pushed off the bonnet to stare.

'Sup, my bredren?' said the whitest of the two shirtless fellows. Virgil was used to this kind of remark—Mum was Afro-Jamaican, Dad was a white Scot. Still, it wasn't a glowing start.

'Sorry, guys,' he wiped the sweat off his top lip, 'Would you mind moving your car? It's just, my mum needs room to get into her wheelchair and there's nowhere else to—'

'Are you hearing this, Jonesy?' the square-headed one with the goatee leaned in through the car window, 'Django Unchained here wants us to move.'

'Tell him to scarper.'

'Yeah, push off, you little nonce,' said the other skinhead, fiddling with his earring. 'Before you get hurt.'

'No,' Virgil stood his ground.

'Didn't you hear me? Go!'

'I'm not moving, you don't have the right to park here.' Virgil could scarcely believe the words coming out of his mouth. *Sign me up for the Darwin awards.* His head was screaming at him to cut his losses and get out of there. But in his heart, he felt justified. There was no need for the Saxo to be there, any reasonable person would apologise and move. These were not reasonable people, though. He knew that before he stepped out of his mum's little red Corsa. But Virgil believed that if everyone kept silent about injustice—however trivial—then nothing would ever change. It was right to stand your ground. It was right to…

'OOF!' the lad with the earring punched him in the stomach. Virgil nearly fell to the ground, only his outstretched fingertips saved him from the gum-spattered tarmac. Before he could straighten up, discount Michael Peña had got him in a full-nelson. There was a moment where Virgil looked at them and they looked at him. *Look at those teeth, these guys must be brothers.* Then the two skinheads took it in turns to pummel his body.

'Stop! Stop it! Somebody help! Please, somebody call the police!'

Mum. Virgil barely recognised her animal screams as she struggled across the car park to his defence. *How did she get out of the car and into her wheelchair, which was on the back seat!?*

'Leave him alone, you THUGS!' Zelda pushed at Michael Peña's back, almost losing balance and having to quickly right the wheelchair. 'Get off him! Get off before I, before I…' she lost steam, sobbing at her own helplessness.

Square-Head gave Virgil one last blow to the jaw, making it feel as if it had come away on his knuckles. Then he said, 'Turn him around, Benji, I'm taking Mummy for a spin!'

Virgil roared his fury as the block-headed youth in tracksuit bottoms and Nike Airs flicked up the handles on his mother's wheelchair and began to push her. Zelda McAllister didn't scream or even shout for help. It was plain from her wide eyes and crumpled mouth that she was terrified. She didn't like being pushed at the best of times, and even then, she would only let Virgil or his dad do it. As they began to go in tighter and tighter circles, narrowly avoiding parked cars, Zelda tried in vain to put her scissor brakes on. This only resulted in her catching her fingers in the spokes and crying out in agony as they snapped.

Square-Head didn't stop though. Faster and faster he went, his face lit up with taboo-breaking glee. Virgil screamed and squirmed and pleaded until he was close to passing out. The thug's forearm dug into his chin and the bulging bicep was cutting off most of his air supply. He could feel his captor shaking with laughter as Zelda was spun to and fro. It was like some sick performance of swan lake. Virgil twisted to see the other skinhead, bent double, tears running down his gaunt face and dripping off his yellow teeth. There was even a sliver of snot coming out where he couldn't contain his snorts of laughter.

Virgil strained further to see inside the Saxo. Two skull-patterned arms rested on the steering wheel, holding a phone. *He's filming it, he's actually filming it!*

Filled with fresh rage, Virgil kicked and elbowed, trying desperately to break free. The strong arm wouldn't budge. So, Virgil bit it. He chomped down hard and felt the blood bubble up around his lips. His teeth went in so far that he was surprised not to have a chunk of the guy's arm in his mouth when he let go, bellowing like a downed bison.

'You little freak!' he pushed Virgil into a van in the next bay, knocking his head against the wing mirror. 'You little—' he stared for a moment at the oozing crescent on his forearm, then advanced with murder in his eyes.

'That's enough!' A stick came down with a sharp crack on the thug's shoulder. 'The police are coming, I'd suggest you stop before you do something you *really* regret.' Virgil spat sticky red onto the floor. From where he was standing, he could only see socks in sandals and the green velvet of corduroy. *Pastor Jerome?*

'Make a move, old man,' Michael Peña growled as he rubbed the bite mark. He started at the pensioner but the walking stick whistled around again, this time cracking off his skull. Now bleeding from two places, he retreated and got into the Saxo. Skull sleeves revved the engine.

Across the car park, Square-Head looked up. Getting the hint, he sprinted back with Zelda, making formula one noises as he weaved in and out of the bike racks. Then he tipped her out in a huge puddle that had accumulated next to the trolleys.

The Saxo backed out at speed, knocking into Zelda's wheelchair and sending it careering into a family who stood watching open-mouthed. The two remaining lads jumped in through the rear doors and the car screeched away—a violent blue blur that gleamed as it broke free of the concrete shade and raced through red lights onto the open road.

CHAPTER TWO

SELF-PRESERVATION

After the Saxo had gone, Pastor Jerome helped Virgil lift Zelda out of the puddle and back into her chair. The Quickie Helium didn't seem damaged, *that wheelchair has been worth every penny*, but Zelda had bruised her palms in the fall.

'It's days like these when you're glad you can't feel half your body!' she chirped as she sat soggily on her cushion, dirty water still running off the backs of her legs and spotting the floor. Zelda's fingers hurt too much for her to propel herself back to the car, so Virgil pushed her. When they got there, she unlocked it to find Maisie happily fiddling with the sun-blind on her window.

'Apple? Nack?' she inquired—they always took some fruit to keep her occupied in the shop.

Maisie was gnawing on a browning core by the time the police arrived. Zelda was all for staying and describing the men who had assaulted them, 'Get our statements while the details are still fresh, I can manage on ibuprofen.'

But the decision was made for her, hospital first—the interview could wait.

~ ~ ~

Forty minutes later, Virgil and Maisie were homebound in their dad's car. They had dropped Mum at Oldley General Hospital, where she insisted on being left and instructed them all to go home and get some dinner. Maisie slept while Virgil filled his father in. Zelda, it appeared, had not been very forthcoming on the phone, so Tony McAllister was keen to get the whole story.

'What do you mean you didn't get a look at them? They had you in a headlock for goodness sake!'

'It all happened so quickly, Dad, plus I was looking at Mum most of the time. The guys who did it were… they were just ordinary! I wouldn't blink if I saw them on a street corner, or skulking down the back of Thornes.' Thornes was a local-carpenters with a secluded rear porch where village kids would trade low-grade weed and show each other pocket-knives they'd bought online.

'Mum said they'd pushed her around a bit, is that what happened?' His dad's knuckles were bone-white on the steering wheel.

'It was awful. I couldn't move, I could only watch. He was going so fast, I thought he was going to ram her into a wall or a car or… Dad, could you slow down please?'

'Scum,' Dad braked a little, 'abominable, damnable scum. I mean, who *does* that? To a woman too! I tell you what, Virgil, and you know I'm against violence, but if I'd have been there, I'd have… I'd have…' he inhaled, too riled up to put into words the visceral beatings he was imagining.

'I know, Dad. You'd have protected her.'

His father nodded, vindicated. 'You're a good boy, you've got your mum's fire in you that's for sure. But you need your old man's cool head,' he tapped his temple as they pulled up outside the family's two-bedroom bungalow.

'Dad…' Virgil figured this would be a sore point, but it would soon come out anyway. Tony shifted his weight slightly to look at his son. Virgil tugged on an earlobe, 'The attack on Mum and me, it wasn't unprovoked.'

'What do you mean? Of course, it was!'

'No. I kind of—well, there was nowhere for us to park, there never is, and Mum had been driving around for ages looking and then, well, I got out of the car and asked these lads to move. And that's when it all kicked off.'

Maisie was stirring, she kicked her pudgy legs, a shoe hanging off her cotton sock by a Velcro strap. Dad massaged the steering wheel while he processed this new piece of information. He was weighing his next words carefully, Virgil had seen him do it before.

'You know I'm proud of you. That's not up for discussion. You're the man of the house now, and you lead by example. And there's a part of me that agrees with you. It *isn't* right. It isn't *ever* right that people disrespect those who are weaker than themselves. And, Virgil, if by some miracle you were the indestructible man,' he punched his son's arm playfully, 'then I would say, "go get 'em!" But the reality is, your mum needs you. Maisie needs you. Who's going to look after them if you get yourself busted up in some intensive care unit or worse? Son, when you have people under your care, self-preservation is the name of the game. It has to be. There are going to be times when you will have to walk away because that is survival.'

Walk away? Like you walked away from us? Virgil wanted to say it but his jaw throbbed and his body ached too much for a round of verbal sparring with his dad. He took his father's advice and said nothing. Maisie let out a disgruntled cry. Tony rapped the dashboard, satisfied that his lecture had been received loud and clear. Virgil got out, slamming the door with more force than was necessary.

As Tony carried a bleary-eyed Maisie over the threshold, Virgil stood boiling in the lounge. The worst thing wasn't that he had been hurt standing up for his mum—he would wear his purple jaw like a badge of honour. The worst thing was that his father was right. If he stood any chance of surviving long enough to look after his family, then next time he would have to let the injustice slide.

Face it, you're a weed and you always will be.

~ ~ ~

The tears ran hot and wet down Virgil's swollen face as he talked.

'I know it sounds stupid but I can't remember,' he forced down great gulps, 'they were in a blue Saxo, that's all.'

'Nothing about how they were dressed, how they looked?'

One of them looked like Michael Peña, how ridiculous does that sound?

'The two that hit me had their shirts off.'

'Any distinctive tattoos? Accessories?'

Yeah, one's got my front teeth embedded in his arm.

Some images were coming back. 'Yes, actually, the driver had skulls in a twisting vine on both forearms, you know, the thorny kind, like around Sleeping Beauty's castle type thing.'

The officer, a large blonde man squeezed awkwardly onto a kitchen stool, glanced up from his notepad. A trickle of sweat rolled silently over a protruding vein on his forehead. Seeing that Virgil was serious about the tattoos, he wrote "skulls, Sleeping Beauty vines" on his pad.

'Is there anything else, did they speak to each other at all, use any names?'

'I can't remember. Mum?' Virgil bit his tongue to ward off the untameable urge to bawl. Zelda said she was sorry but she didn't hear any names.

The policeman's hard grey eyes softened, 'You don't need to be sorry. You've been through quite the ordeal.' He lowered his voice, 'Now, Virgil, I'm probably meant to leave telling you to stay safe and avoid confrontations like this in the future. But for what it's worth, I think what you did was very brave. Just make sure you've got a backup plan next time.'

'Thanks,' Virgil dried his eyes on his t-shirt sheepishly. 'Could I have some water, please? I feel like I can still taste… y'know.'

'It's your house, mate!' The officer shifted so that Virgil could get to the sink. The water was so cold it hurt his head. He swilled around several gulps and spat them out, then rubbed fresh palmfuls all over his lips, desperately trying to cleanse himself. It was agony; his cheek was all puffy and one eye had been forced shut by the swelling.

He sat down, pressing his hands into the table to stop them trembling, 'What happens next?'

'Well, we'll pull the CCTV from the car park and take a look at it. See if we can identify them that way. Then we'll interview the other witnesses.' Officer Blonde sucked his gums. 'That's about it for now. But we've got your number, so we'll be in touch.' He breathed deeply, then offered Virgil his hand. 'Good to meet you, son, I'm sorry you got mixed up in all this. Mrs McAllister, how're those fingers doing?'

Zelda McAllister had been shaken but lucid while the policeman took his statements. She had even cracked a joke about losing her shopping list. She didn't cry until Officer Blonde left.

'I'm so useless in this thing. I could've stopped them before... but now I'm just... just...'

'Mum, stop it. You couldn't have stopped them before. There were four of them.'

'Maybe, but they might've taken me seriously.'

CHAPTER THREE

PINK FLOYD

Despite Mum's insistence that she was proud of him, guilt crouched at Virgil's door like a stray cat. He wished that he was stronger, faster, tougher. More than a pushover.

Zelda had returned from the hospital with her fingers taped. She didn't complain, she even apologised for not cooking. Mum had always been feisty, and since her spinal injury, it was like the extrovert inside had taken over. He supposed that this was a good thing. Zelda's 'can-do' Jamaican spirit was alive and kicking, even if her legs weren't. Sure, there were tough days—moments of frustration and sadness. But Virgil had the good sense to ride these out rather than book her a psychiatrist.

He stirred the jerk chicken as it crackled away in the pan, it was a meal they often fell back on if Zelda was late home from work. In she came with Maisie on her knee.

'I'll take over if you do your sister's nappy,' she said. 'Sorry, I'm just finding it tricky with the—' she waved her clump of fingers.

'Course!' Virgil washed his hands and took off the apron. Grabbing Maisie under her arms, he swung her around the kitchen, her giggling face so close to his, everything else a blur.

'Not too rough!' Zelda chided.

Maisie squealed with happiness.

'Oh, boy. Maisie, you stink!'

Later, as he stepped out to bin the conspicuously warm nappy bag, Virgil glimpsed a white hat bobbing down the cut-through at the back of their garden. *I know that hat.* It was the man he had christened 'Pink Floyd'. He had named him so because of the faded Dark Side of the Moon T-shirt that stretched over his protruding belly. He had no idea what the man's real name was, but the burst blood vessels on his dewlaps more than justified the Pink pseudonym. Every afternoon, Virgil would walk up the alleyway on his way home from school. And every day, without fail, Pink Floyd would be ambling along, a book tucked under his arm and his little Jack Russell trotting along behind.

Virgil had been brought up to be polite to strangers, especially elderly ones. He would always greet Floyd with a buoyant 'Hello,' or 'Afternoon,' and the warmest smile he could muster. Every single time, he would receive nothing back. Not a nod of the head or a wink of the eye. The rosy-cheeked prog-rocker just kept plodding as if Virgil were no more than an autumn leaf. Rather than be offended, Virgil found this quite amusing and would sometimes daydream about breaking the cycle—causing Pink Floyd to acknowledge his existence. He had greeted him in fifteen different languages now, and had even gone in for the handshake, the fist-bump and the high-five, all to no avail. He sometimes imagined drop-kicking the Jack Russell into a back garden. *The old git would notice me then!* He would never really do it, but a boy could dream.

He slammed the lid on the dustbin, recoiling from the accumulated stench of nappies warmed all day by the sun. The white hat dipped out of sight. *I wonder what old grumpy guts is up to tonight.* Virgil had never seen him out so late and felt a sudden urge to follow, but Maisie's crying snapped him back to reality, so he stepped back inside the bungalow.

Zelda was very independent for someone with her level of injury—or so the occupational therapists said. Despite this, there were still many things that other mums did that she simply couldn't do. Now that his dad was gone, these tasks fell to Virgil. He never grumbled, not to his mum, not to anyone. *It's not her fault that she can't get out of the shower, or that she needs help with toileting and dressing. If she could do it herself, she would. And as she can't, I will. After all, she washed, dressed and changed me when I couldn't do it!* This was Virgil's philosophy. It was what he reminded himself of at 2 AM when Zelda called for help rolling over in bed. Or in the pre-school rush as he scrambled to get Maisie fed and put Zelda's work clothes on her. It wasn't the life he'd expected, but he hated the idea of someone else doing it for her. Once you got used to it, it just became normal. A new normal.

Very occasionally, Virgil had his own moments of bleakness. They snuck up unexpectedly, wrapping him in thin tendrils of melancholy. Sometimes, he felt a boiling anger that he couldn't diffuse, except to go into the garden and kick a ball around very hard. One time, he just left Zelda and Maisie and ran until his lungs ached and his mouth tasted like copper. Some days, Virgil would feel a crushing sadness. He wondered what kind of life awaited Maisie. Whether Dad would ever come back. How long Mum would live now. Zelda usually coaxed him out of these moods. She could read him like a magazine.

'Don't you be getting burdened about me! The Lord knows my days. Those who honour me, I will honour. That's a promise. And our God keeps his promises.'

Sometimes, just before sleep, Virgil would fantasise about confronting the man who had put his mum in the chair. What would he say to him? *Do* to him? Would he be able to control himself? Would all this raw anger come bursting out? He knew that his dad had tracked the punk down early on, but what had come of their interaction he never found out and was too scared to ask.

Mum and Maisie didn't make a peep that night. But Virgil lay awake, massaging his tender stomach and trying to work his pillow into a less-agonising shape. He tried to picture the assailants from the car park. Various ogre-like contortions drifted across the ceiling. He knew he could identify all four if he saw them again, but what was the likelihood of that happening?

I wish I was strong, I wish I was fast, I wish I was indestructible.

I wish.

CHAPTER FOUR

ST JUSTUS' CHURCH OF
THE MARTYRS

The next day was Sunday. And for Zelda, that meant one thing: Church. The McAllisters attended the village Anglican—St Justus' Church of the Martyrs—which was presided over by Pastor Jerome Yeboah—the same Pastor Jerome who had rescued Virgil in the car park yesterday. Jerome was a North African man whose warm hands and fiery sermons were the subject of many a rapturous lunchtime dissection by Zelda. Virgil liked Jerome and the people at St Justus. They were always friendly to him.

The Derbyshire village of Prestley was built on a large hill. The McAllister's bungalow was situated on a 1960s estate near the bottom where things flattened out, while St Justus pierced the sky from the hill's highest point. At the far side of St Justus, a little beyond the churchyard, all the roads and footpaths came to an abrupt end. A grassy knoll rolled out towards the horizon, offering a spectacular view of the woodlands, but also a swift death to anyone who tiptoed too close to the edge. This precipice was known as Widow's Peak. Prestley's main road was a wide avenue of shops and businesses that cut a straight line up the centre of the village. Because of its twenty-two-degree gradient, some inventive soul had named it Steep Street. The McAllisters normally walked up Steep Street to get to church, Maisie on Zelda's knee with Virgil pushing. It was one hell of a climb.

As he arrived at the top of Prestley, perspiring in the fresh morning air, Virgil helped his mum up the trickiest part of the slope that led from the road and through the graveyard. Maisie was on Zelda's knee and squealed, 'Eyes! Eyes!' as the rising sun dazzled them. St Justus' Church of the Martyrs leaned out protectively, casting a long triangle of shade across the path. The grass was still dew-soaked where the spire's shadow had denied the sun. The three of them blinked as their eyes adjusted to the gloom, then the heavy door whined on its hinges and Mrs Duckett, the squat choir mistress, beckoned them inside.

'Hello, Zelda, oh!' the corners of her mouth went down as she inhaled sharply, 'Virgil, what happened to your face?'

He shuffled forward, looking at the flagstones, and mumbled, 'Got beat up.'

'Sorry to hear it. I hope they got what they deserved,' Mrs Duckett blushed, clearly realising that this sentiment wasn't in line with the church's teaching. She recovered well, turning to Maisie. 'And who is this?' she bent and pointed to Mr Biggles, the rabbit teddy.

'Biggles!' shouted Maisie.

Everyone fawned, especially the old couple behind them. Virgil turned back to ask how Mrs Farrow's hip operation had gone, but was completely distracted by a strange sight. To the side of the 13th-century church lay two large wooden doors, they were framed in stone and fractionally raised from the verdure. Glazed black by time and covered in vines, the doors to the crypt had always made Virgil uneasy. They reminded him of a trapdoor. He used to imagine them opening—red light pouring forth as some poor bystander leaving flowers on a grave was dragged into the depths. He had even dreamed about them, his legs betraying him, walking willingly inside as the doors creaked open.

It wasn't the crypt itself that had caught Virgil's attention. Lying a little to the right of the ancient doors was... Pink Floyd's fishing hat... or one virtually identical. *Strange!*

'Well, I suppose we had better go in,' Mr Farrow said tentatively. Virgil saw that a queue had formed behind them.

'Yes, sorry. I… I was just...' He stole one last look at the hat, *surely, it's not his,* then passed through the door, shaking Mrs Duckett's hand.

St Justus was unique for a church of its time. Not exactly a monastery but not a traditional village chapel either, it was something in between. Like a half-scale cathedral with all the requisite towers and secret passages. Great white pillars held up the vaulted ceiling where pin-pricks of light shone through a thousand stars, carved into the dark wood. It was well-known that an intricate system of polished glass in the roof allowed the light to penetrate in this way. When he was younger, Virgil could never understand why the stars didn't drip on them all when it was raining. He had been up the bell tower a handful of times since the wooden staircase had been restored; the view of Prestley and its surrounding countryside was stunning. On a clear day, you could even see the Spindles—angular columns of rock which crowned the hills to the far north.

There would often be visitors—Americans who had come to puzzle over a church this size being built in such a small village. The occasional historian writing a thesis on the mysterious St Justus. Pastor Jerome (he preferred Pastor over Reverend, after his free-church background) was the reigning authority on such matters. And although Virgil usually switched off during his fiery yet overly-sentimental sermons, he did like to hear Jerome talk about the stained glass.

St Justus' stained glass windows were another aspect of its distinct peculiarity. Untouched since the thirteenth century, they showed scenes from the book of Revelation. The remarkable thing about them was that they depicted people of all nations—black, white, and everything in between—joining together to fight the hordes of evil.

As he found his seat next to Maisie, Virgil slouched in the pew and gazed up at his favourite window. A man with an afro, wearing a shining suit of armour, faced off against a towering black dragon. The man had wings on his heels like a Greek-god and held a flaming yellow sword. Virgil had loved this window ever since he was a child, and used to plead with his parents to sit at the front so he could be close to it. He liked to imagine that the man in armour was him, and the vivid imagery surrounding this unusual scene only fuelled his imagination when Pastor Jerome got boring. *How many stained-glass windows in the country have a guy with an afro fighting a dragon?*

Virgil ran a hand over his own hair, trimmed back to nothing after the taunting at school. He didn't like it this short, but he liked it more than the constant heckling on the bus and the people who launched stationery at him, trying to get things stuck in it. Come to think of it, his new haircut hadn't solved that issue at all—now the pencils and protractors just bounced off his skull. At least the afro had provided some cushioning.

As the service dragged on, Virgil couldn't stop thinking about the hat by the crypt. As they stood for hymns and sat for psalms, he pondered its unlikely arrival. Had Pink Floyd come up to the graveyard last night? If so, why had he left his hat? Virgil had never seen him without it. Perhaps he was in a hurry? *You're being paranoid, I bet loads of men his age own a hat like that. It has been a windy week, some visitor just got it blown off, that's all.*

He tuned in to Pastor Jerome.

'...ever since God laid down the law for Moses, there has been provision for the fatherless and the widow. But this is not an onerous must-do, my brothers and sisters, far from it! We were all of us adopted into God's family the second we trusted the Saviour, and as we serve and protect the vulnerable in our community, we partner with the Almighty himself. This is joyful work, my friends!' Pastor

Jerome beamed his gappy-pearly-whites at the congregation.

After the service ended, Virgil made a hasty exit, partly to avoid questions about his pulverised face, but mainly to scout out the crypt entrance. The hat lay as it had done before, a few paces from the undercroft. There were no other signs of disturbance, but the long grass beneath the cherry tree had been flattened.

Virgil picked up the hat, turning it over in his hands. Were those flecks of blood on the brim? He flipped it over and found that, written crudely in marker, a name was just visible: Floyd Burlock. Something fell out of the inside band. A thin slip of paper. It had been folded many times over but now expanded to show a spidery scrawl. Virgil unfurled the tiny message. It read: SHE FOUND IT BUT WON'T SHARE. UNLIMITED POWER LIVES WITHIN THE CRYPT.

CHAPTER FIVE

BULWARK

'What is your relationship to Mr Burlock?' the police officer asked, rubbing the five-o'clock shadow on his dimpled chin. He had a coffee stain on his white shirt and his badge was pinned on almost diagonally. James Siddons, it read.

'We don't have a relationship. I walk past him every day.' Virgil leaned forward in his seat. 'It's actually really weird because I didn't know his real name before, but I'd nicknamed him Pink Floyd because of this T-shirt he wears.' He could see that he was losing the man. 'I'm concerned about him—that's why I brought it in.'

'OK,' Officer Siddons clicked away. 'And it was just the hat? Nothing else left behind? No wallet? Bag?'

Should I mention the cryptic note? I don't want him to think this is a wind-up. 'No, just the hat.'

'Right,' Officer Siddons made a few more clicks, his hand drifting over a worn Hot Fuzz mouse-mat. Virgil wasn't sure whether this filled him with confidence or not, but at least it meant he had a sense of humour. 'I've logged it on the system,' Siddons swivelled his chair, 'but I can't file it under missing persons until we've investigated ourselves. What I'll do is send a bobby round to Mr Burlock's this evening, see if we can't clear it up. The blood is troubling, not because it's blood per se—I mean, you could cut your finger gardening and smear it on your nice white hat—it's the spray effect that I don't like. So, I'll be sending this off to the lab for analysis.' He waved the sealed bag with the mysterious hat inside.

'Now, you wanted to ask about something else?'

'Yes, please,' Virgil clapped his hands together. 'It's unrelated. I only wanted to ask if you had made any progress with the CCTV of the guys who did this?' He gestured to his plum eye and mottled cheek. Officer Siddons leaned right back in his chair.

'Not that I know of. Although I'm not the person handling your case, that's Officer Kaplan. She's not in today.'

'No problem, thanks for your time.' Virgil went to leave, then turned back at the door, 'I appreciate you taking me seriously.'

Officer Siddons gave a half-smile and thumbs up, then his glasses reflected the screen again. Virgil bowed his head respectfully, 'Thanks again.' He backed out of the room.

Zelda was waiting in the car with Maisie.

'Any joy?'

'Not really,' Virgil slumped into the passenger seat. 'He said it's not a big deal until Burlock is actually missing, but he didn't like the look of the blood.'

'Really?'

'Yeah. It bothered him. Didn't stop shaking his head the whole time he was holding it.'

'Hmm.'

'You don't seem too upset about Floyd Burlock, Mum, what is it about him?'

'Oh, nothing. He has a reputation in the village.'

'Care to be more specific? I mean, are we talking axe murderer or bad driver?'

'No, it's not those. He's... oh, what do I know? He used to come to the church. Let's just say he left under a cloud.'

'He's still a person. He might be hurt.'

'He is, and yes he could be. Leave it with the police.'

Virgil stared out of the window absently, watching the pavement shimmy alongside the moving car. *Who secretes a note in their hat?* Was Burlock some kind of cold-war spy? He pondered the words. SHE FOUND IT BUT WON'T SHARE.

Who was 'she'? And what did she find? UNLIMITED POWER LIVES WITHIN THE CRYPT. Something about this phrase sent Virgil's nerve endings jangling. *Unlimited power. Boy, could I do with a bit of that.* He flipped down the sunshade and pressed the purpling bulge under his right eye.

'We're fragile, aren't we?'

'What do you mean?' Zelda gave a cyclist a wide berth.

'Us. Humans. We break easily. Doesn't take much, one wrong move and you're a goner. Misjudge a rooftop or a traffic light…'

Zelda was quiet for a moment. Then she said, 'Sometimes being fragile makes something more valuable.'

~ ~ ~

'Touch me again, sir, and I'll have you locked up, pedo.'

Bulwark Academy. A breeding ground for the physical equivalent of the internet troll, and Virgil's school for the last four years. One never felt safe at Bulwark. You had to be on your guard all the time. So far, Virgil had managed to keep his head down, following Tony's advice. There were racial slurs most days and, of course, the ducking of sharp objects in Maths. 'Aww, Virgil, why'd you shave your head? How are we going to play afro-darts now?' Compared to some of the other abuse going on around him, Virgil felt he was getting off lightly. This week alone he had witnessed yoghurt being poured into a girl's hood, two fights where older students had ganged up on younger ones, one firecracker in assembly, and, the talking point of the week, a year 11 girl's underwear being hoisted up the flag-pole. How they got hold of it was still a matter of speculation.

Virgil had always been a target—his skin had determined that for him. So, he became a social ghost, all the time visualising the karmic demise of every last sucker-punching one of them. He let his eyes bore into the bullies, recording every cruel word, measuring every spiteful action, and praying that a way could exist for him to level the scales. *Unlimited power lives within the crypt.*

Today he would break his father's rule into a thousand tiny pieces.

CHAPTER SIX
A PROMISE KEPT

Joshua Brown had Down's Syndrome. He was pudgy with badly-gelled brown hair, and he spoke in a high voice with a lisp. Virgil liked him a lot. When Joshua arrived at Bulwark Academy, everyone had taken one look and written him off: 'dead meat.' But despite the relentless attacks, the teasing and name-calling, Joshua had stayed. This earned him tremendous respect, Virgil's included. He had been looking for a way to get to know Joshua when he and his family moved into one of the council houses opposite.

One evening, Joshua's Mum, Louise, had come over to ask Zelda whether Virgil would mind walking Joshua to and from the bus stop.

'He does dawdle and gets easily distracted and disorientated,' she had explained. 'Oh, and we don't *expect* Virgil to do it.' Louise Brown had stood wringing her hands, 'We know that there's a lot of negativity around learning difficulties, so we will understand if Virgil doesn't want to be seen with him—'

'Let me stop you there,' Zelda had interrupted, 'VIRGIL!'

Virgil, who had been eavesdropping, sidled up to the front door.

'Darling, this is Louise, Joshua Brown's mum, she's asking if you could walk to the bus stop together?'

'Yeah, fine.'

'Joshua has Down's Syndrome. You'll make sure he's treated fairly, won't you, Virgil?'

'Er, yeah, Mum, of course I will!'

'Promise Louise.'

'Mrs Brown, I promise I'll look out for Joshua.'

It was a promise he sometimes regretted.

'Joshua Brown's got Down's,' sang Daniel Dauber.

'Hello, Joshua Down's,' parroted the dumb voice of Keegan Rice. He threw a tennis ball which bounced off Joshua's head as he hurried past. *Where on earth is his support worker?* thought Virgil.

'Is he crying?' mocked Ben 'Pidge' Pidgeon.

'No,' said Dauber loudly. 'Down's can't cry, it's genetically impossible.'

'I've heard you can make a killing selling their tears on eBay!' Pidge boomed.

'eBay,' guffawed Keegan Rice as Pidge slapped him on the back, and high-fived Dauber. At the far end of the corridor, Joshua Brown turned and gave them the finger, then darted out of sight. The taunts stopped like a power-cut.

'Did you—'

'Did you see—'

'Did he just?'

The three boys thundered after Joshua.

Virgil groaned, tightening his bag straps. *I made your mum a promise. Joshua, you are going to get us both killed!* He tore after them.

Virgil was light on his feet. It was one of the things he liked most about himself. As his school shoes pounded the thin carpet, he tried to predict where Joshua might go. The English corridor backed onto an IT Suite surrounded by glass windows, it was empty, save for a few students. There was no way Joshua had made it around the whole lot and out of the far door unseen, and unless he had ducked behind the half-wall…

Virgil stopped outside the boys' toilets. The gap under the door betrayed a sliver of fluorescence, *those lights are motion-sensitive.* He let Dauber, Rice and Pidge storm past the English rooms, shouldering each other and cornering badly. They clattered out of the fire exit, forcing a gaggle of girls to huddle together with playful shrieks. Virgil waited a couple of beats, then slipped inside the toilets. He couldn't believe that anyone would go for a dead-end hiding place like this, but then, this was Joshua we were talking about. Sure enough, there were his square shoes under the middle cubicle. He hadn't even thought to stand on a toilet seat. *How have you survived so long?*

'Josh?'

'Virgil?'

The cubicle unlocked and out he came, beetroot and panting. He loosened his badly-knotted tie.

'I was being chased by D-d-d-d-daniel D-d-d—'

'I know. They're gone. Ran straight into the quiet garden.'

'Oh,' Joshua leant on a sink, splashing water onto his face and all over the floor. He straightened up, doing his hair in the mirror and adjusting the little gold chain he wore. Seeing Virgil's reflection, he said, 'How come you're in here?'

'I was following you, you complete doughnut! Look, I've got History and you have?'

'R.E.'

'So, let's get out of here before they come back.'

The door banged open, framing Dauber, Rice and Pidge like some hideous Picasso.

'Look who we have here! Lovers in the bathroom,' Dauber advanced.

'Go on, Deej,' urged Pidge, who was sweating like a stuck pig. (DJ or Deej was Dauber's nickname, borne out of his first two names: Daniel and Jude. Virgil made a point of always calling him Daniel, much to Dauber's annoyance, and refused to buy into this idea that Bulwark's big bad should be venerated with a cool moniker).

'Put your fists down, Daniel,' said Virgil. 'Joshua doesn't want a fight, and I've got History. Come on, just let us go.'

'How about I put you in a wheelchair like your mum?'

Dauber lurched forward with a fist. Virgil dodged and slipped on the wet floor, just managing to hold on to a cubicle. Dauber was not so lucky since he had thrown all his weight behind the punch. His right foot went from under him with a squeak and brought all his considerable bulk crashing onto the sink where Joshua had been splashing his face. The ceramic basin remained intact but Dauber's temple came up like a ping pong ball. Seizing his moment, almost instinctively, Virgil stamped down hard on Dauber's ribs. He felt them break under his foot like treading on a sack full of coat-hangers. Dauber lay still, staring vacantly at the apple-sourz green of the wall.

Pidge ran at Virgil, bellowing. He too skidded on the tiles, his loose shoelaces flapping. Stopping miraculously, he grabbed Virgil around the collar and started squeezing.

'Joshua, kkkk,' gasped Virgil, 'Joshua, g-gak help kkkk!'

Joshua stood motionless with Dauber at his feet. A couple of times he rocked on his heels as if he were coming to help, but stayed put, eyes like pineapple rings and his head shaking imperceptibly. Virgil noticed that his white school shirt was see-through where he had splashed water on it. *If the last sight I see on earth is Joshua Brown's nipples!*

Fighting for air as he was, Virgil could not escape the pungent detail of everything Pidge had eaten for lunch, some of which was still smeared on his chin. His vision wobbled—dark-blue blotches appeared on his sight like a damaged reel of film. His hands were wrapped around

Pidge's, trying desperately to relieve the crushing. He couldn't see what Keegan Rice was doing.

As it turned out, the second Dauber's ribs cracked like a bundle of twigs, Keegan Rice had flown down the corridor shouting. Finding the first two classrooms empty, he had grabbed Mr Deacon, a wiry young teacher, by the sleeve and dragged him to the toilets.

Meanwhile, Virgil, having no idea that help was on its way, let go of Pidge with one hand and dug around in his pockets for something, anything that could alleviate the bursting pressure on his windpipe. Finding nothing but a crumpled bus-pass and a pack of chewing gum in his own pockets, he reached into Pidge's tight-fitting trousers. *A pencil! Blunt though, typical Pidge.* He held it in his fist with his thumb over the red nubbin, and began to press. Ben Pidgeon's eyes popped, as the pencil—blunt as it was—entered just under his ribcage and sank into the soft of his belly, taking his unpierced shirt with it. His hands weakened and he released Virgil, who sank to the floor retching. Pidge staggered back onto the mirrors, gaping at his stomach. The pencil stuck out at a downward angle, quivering. There was no blood, just the yellow and black of the thin instrument and the LER HB 2 of STAEDTLER HB 2.

The door was flung open and Mr Deacon stumbled in, looking like an anorexic ghost. His mouth did a rabbity twitch as he laid eyes on Dauber's body, then hung wide open as he caught sight of the pencil in Pidge.

'Holy Mackerel,' he said, then fainted.

CHAPTER SEVEN

EXCLUSION

They drove in silence. From the bonnet, a miniature heat-haze distorted the horizon, making everything vacillate from where Virgil slouched in the passenger seat.

'Three weeks,' Zelda broke the stalemate. 'What will you do with yourself?'

Virgil grunted.

'I suppose they'll send work home for you.'

'Mum, I don't want to talk about it right now. Can we please just get Maisie?'

'Yes, sorry, darling. Pam's sent me a picture of her in their paddling pool if you check my phone.' Pam and Mick were their immediate neighbours, a milkman and a cleaner. They had six grown-up children of their own and insisted on child-minding Maisie whenever Zelda needed help. They were good people, though their house smelled strongly of dog. Virgil would always surreptitiously hold his breath whenever he went over. Their black Labrador, Tenzin, was a harmless old thing, but he had a habit of drooling on feet. You never wore flip-flops to Pam and Mick's.

As they drove, the reality of his exclusion began to sink in. What was he going to do? Mum would be at work, Maisie at nursery. *I'll go crazy alone in the house.* They didn't have WIFI at home and Virgil had sold his PlayStation to pay for Maisie to have some new clothes.

As they were coming through Oldley, the luminous green of the Asda storefront crept into view. Virgil got a tightening in his stomach as they drove past the concrete pillars. The sun blasted off the outside of the shelter, making the underneath appear darker than usual. *That place.* The place his unconscious mind had taken him back to every night since the attack. The place he got short of breath just thinking about. *Do the Saxo crew still shop there? Are they laying low? Or do they still swing into the disabled bays like they own the place?* As the supermarket flitted by, Virgil had a brainwave.

'Mum, can you drop me at Wilko, please?

'Sure, I can. What do you need? There's a five-pound note in the glove.'

'Oh, just some fresh deodorant and essentials.'

Duct tape. Stanley knife. Padlocks.

He knew exactly what he would be doing over these next three weeks.

CHAPTER EIGHT

A DISH BEST SERVED WARM

A red Mercedes backed into the disabled bays. Its owner got out, checked her hair in the window, then walked with ease into the store. Virgil waited until no one was looking, then let down her rear tyres. He had gone to the library on Wednesday night and watched a few YouTube tutorials. It was surprisingly easy.

A few minutes later, Ms Mercedes screeched away, not realising her tyres were flat. Half an hour passed. A blue van pulled into the same spot. Virgil reached into the bag for his pliers and waited. Three men got out and walked off. They weren't even going inside! He watched them all the way across the main road and into town, nuggying each other and larking about. *We'll see who's laughing when you get back.* J.M. Barrow and Sons, plasterers, electricians and odd jobs. *Wonder if Gramps knew them?* Virgil knelt with the pretence of tying his lace, then slid out the pliers and hammer and with a few well-placed blows, clamped the van's exhaust pipe completely shut. Virgil didn't see the men return, but he took great pleasure in imagining their faces when they saw his handiwork. Hopefully, the engine would pack in before they noticed.

The first week of being Asda's unofficial car park security was nearly over. Virgil's overarching design was to be on the lookout for the blue Saxo. In the meantime, he couldn't deny a certain amount of satisfaction as he punished the lazy. Friday brought with it the largest number of offenders yet. Dressed in his homemade parking attendant costume, he was speaking to someone what felt like every twenty minutes. Certain times of the day were busier, and so the retribution was more limited. Despite this, that morning, Virgil still managed to puncture the tyres of five sports cars, two Land rovers, a 50CC dirt bike and a beat-up Golf.

Because of the heat, many people arrived with their roof down. Rookie error. These were Virgil's favourite moments because they gave him access to car interiors without the obvious sound of breaking glass. Next to his backpack, he also kept a supply of double cream. When he felt a person was particularly deserving, he would empty a pot onto the driver's seat or windscreen, then watch from the other side of the car park as they flipped out. Most people flew back into the store to complain, some looked around for the culprit or the hidden camera crew, others simply cleaned up the mess and drove off. Their conscience, Virgil hoped, told them they had got what they deserved.

On Friday night, he finished his 'shift' with a move he'd been desperately wanting to pull off. An opportunity presented itself at five minutes to five. Just as he was preparing to ride home, he saw a man parked in a disabled bay with a phone glued to his ear. Virgil waited for him to exit or reach for his blue badge, but neither happened. He didn't recognise the man or the car, so, wanting to be fair, he strolled over. The number plate was personalised: KABIR 01. Something inside told him this man would not be equable.

The man glanced up at Virgil, then turned away and continued his conversation. He was in his early twenties, driving a BMW, and wearing an expensive-looking suit with the collar turned up. *If ever there was a way to advertise that you were a jerk.* Several gold rings glinted on the hand holding the phone. *So, you're rich and entitled, fine. I'm still going to treat you like I treat everyone else.* Virgil tapped on the glass a second time, harder and longer.

The man's voice was muffled.

'Anyway, I gotta go, some idiot's knocking on my window.'

The man pressed the window button and nothing happened—the engine was off. Blowing hot air as if this were Virgil's fault, he made a meal of wrenching the keys from their slot and opening the door.

'What?' he spat acid.

'Good afternoon, sir, are you aware that this is a blue badge space for people with disabilities and mobility problems?' Virgil gestured to the huge sign directly opposite the windscreen. To Virgil's intense embarrassment, the man rummaged in the glove and pulled out a blue badge. He flung it onto the dashboard so hard that it slid over to the far side of the screen.

'Oh, I'm very sorry, sir,' he said, totally flustered at being caught out. *Hold on a minute.* He craned over the bonnet to get a closer look at the badge. It was all scratched up, so much so that the large black lettering was barely visible. 'Actually, sir, can I see it?' The look the man gave him now could have boiled water. He reached across the dashboard, slapping his hand down on the badge and stepped out of the car, jamming it into Virgil's waiting hands.

'I'm disabled. I have a disability.' He fidgeted, moving from foot to foot like a boxer. The badge looked like it had been dragged across sandpaper all the way to the shops. There were two things letting the man's story down. The first was that the badge had clearly expired five years ago. The second was that it belonged to a large white woman.

'This is a picture of you?'

'Yes.'

'This photograph. This obese Caucasian lady, is you?'

The man ran a finger and thumb over his beard. 'It's my wife.'

'Your wife is called Kabir?' Virgil tapped the woman's image.

'It's her car.'

'OK, Kabir. Now, where is *your* blue badge?'

Something snapped and the man stepped up to Virgil.

'Excuse me, sorry, who are *you*? What are you, like sixteen? Who the hell are *you*? Mind your own business.'

Virgil reached inside his jacket and showed his own fake ID. 'Michael Bay, Horizon parking officer, and the issuer of an eighty-pound fine on this lovely vehicle of yours. Move. Your. Car.'

'Gimme that back.' The man made a swipe for the blue badge, but Virgil was faster.

'I'll be holding onto this because I think you found it or stole it.'

The man's chest was rising and falling, his fists clenching and unclenching. His left eye fluttered of its own accord. He made an infinitesimal move forwards, then stopped.

'I'm going shopping.' He slammed the car door, locking it, and began to stride away, then turned and came back towards Virgil, jabbing an angry finger as he spoke, 'You're lucky you're in uniform. Next time I see you, I'll kick your head in! Then we'll see who's disabled.' He rounded a pillar and was gone.

Virgil stood still for a moment. Shocked at the sudden outburst, but even more amazed that he had emerged unscathed. Then he blinked himself out of his reverie and got to work.

By five past five, he was almost done. There was a trolley padlocked to each of the BMW's door handles, duct tape across the windscreen and all four tyres were flat. He had even managed to ram an apple so far up the exhaust that it couldn't be seen anymore. Before his pièce de résistance, Virgil unlocked his bike and leant it against a nearby pillar. *Quick getaway.* Then he cut through the spindly row of trees that shielded the supermarket from the housing estate next door. Hoping his memory had served him correctly, he was overjoyed to see a little red bin fastened to the lamppost opposite the bench where he sat for lunch. Using a stray plastic bag from the hedges, he gloved-up and reached tentatively into the dog-waste bin. *Oh, man.* It was still warm. He tore back through the treeline. KABIR 01 was still there. *Well, duh, he won't be going anywhere in a hurry with those trolleys.* There was no sign of the big man himself. This had to be done quickly. Virgil did a cursory sweep to check no one was watching, then elbowed the glass on the driver's side as hard as he could. The window remained intact, unlike his elbow, which felt as though it had been split by a chisel. Ignoring the searing pain, he took a couple of steps back and kicked the window, once, twice. It caved in on the fourth kick, the sound tinkling off the grey walls. Virgil tore a hole in the black bag and emptied the contents onto the driver's seat. One piece rolled under the accelerator. *Ugh. A little present for the man who has everything.* He pulled out the stolen blue badge, most of the woman's name was scratched off except for MAN. He guessed that she was Mandy and not Manfred. He turned the badge to look at the sabotaged BMW. *This one's for you, Mandy.*

The ride home was exhilarating. His calves burned like lactic pressure cookers but he cycled hard until he was well clear of the supermarket. The streets cleared and the rush-hour buzz became the winding back road that snaked through the fields towards Prestley. He coasted along the familiar paths that led home. As the adrenaline started to wear off, Virgil began to wrestle with his actions. *I got that guy good. Didn't I? Come on, if anyone deserved it, he did! But did he? Maybe he'd just had a rough day. Maybe he was stressed or recently bereaved. Maybe he was just an entitled loser.* At the time, he had felt completely justified wrecking KABIR 01's day. But now, doubt was settling like a layer of ash, choking out the smouldering desire for vengeance. By the time he was walking his bike down the side of the bungalow, he felt dreadful. *I am not cut out for this.*

Zelda got home just as Virgil was locking the back door. As he helped her out of the car, he sensed a coldness in her. Something wasn't right. Over tea, it came to a head.

'Good day then?' Zelda twiddled her fork endlessly in the midst of her spaghetti, never bringing it to her lips.

'Yep, just working mostly.'

'Nice lunch?'

'Yeah, had soup and… why are you looking at me like that? What's the matter?'

She let the fork drop.

'I came home for lunch today to give you some company.'

Virgil speared a meatball, trying to keep his hand steady.

'What time? I mean, I did pop out for a quick walk about twelve.'

'Twelve 'til one. I ate alone. For an hour. Are you even doing the work they set you?'

'Mum, I am. You can check it, it's all up to date, it's done.'

'I called you. I called you again and again.'

'You know I'm usually good with my phone. Don't give me grief the one time I didn't pick up.'

'Then I called around the neighbours. Do you know what Diane from number seventy-one said? She said she saw you leave on your bike at nine AM. Nine!'

'Diane's a nosey curtain-twitcher.'

'Virgil, what's gotten into you? Fights at school and then this? Sneaking out when you're already suspended? Who were you with?'

'Muuum, I went to the postie for some sweets.'

'You went to buy sweets for four hours? Who were you with?'

'I swear I wasn't *with* anyone. Come on, it's so boring staying home all day.'

'Well, you had better get used to it.' Zelda downed her drink in one. 'You're grounded.'

CHAPTER NINE

TREVOR LEE

The breeze whistling over the headstones made him shiver. His whole back was damp with sweat. Bats danced in the dark above him, he felt the tiny changes in the air from their wings. To his right, Prestley slumbered, blanketed in shadow. To his left, the Manse, a façade of peeling paint. Confused not to find his bedsheet tangled around him, he patted himself down to find jeans and a jacket. *No, no, no, no, nonononono.*

He dug his toes into the sodden turf. His eyes were wide open.

So were the crypt doors.

The sight of it made Virgil draw breath with an inward shriek: two five-pence pieces reflected the pale moonlight back at him. The crypt entrance was soot-black but for the eyes. Virgil had not noticed them at first. He was still in shock to find himself there. Wide with inhuman emphasis, the eerie peepers stared out at him while he stood rooted to the grass. He rubbed his eyes. The crypt doors were closed and the eyes were gone.

Suddenly, adrenaline flooded his paralysed body and he turned heel. He tore down Steep Street, past Tewke's Butchers and Frank's Bakery, diagonally over the crossing by Dinah's tea rooms. All the properties lay empty, the occasional uplighter teasing macabre shadows from pot plants and desktops. His bare feet made a hollow plap, plap, plap as he ran, but he paid them no regard. They pounded the pavements with one aim: get as far away from the crypt as possible.

Finding the front door open, Virgil darted inside and locked it, being careful not to peer through the mottled glass in case anything was peering back. As he crawled into bed, desperately rubbing his cold shoulders and bunching up his toes in the duvet, he pictured those eyes floating towards his bedside in the gloom. He shivered all over. *There must have been a face, there had to have been a face beneath them.*

It took a long time to stop shaking. As the paranoia began to seep away, Virgil found himself beset by a new fear: sleep. How could he trust his unconscious body not to wander back up there? *Unlimited power lives within the crypt. What is going on? Was I wandering up there in search of something? Power? Was Floyd Burlock having crypt dreams too?* Virgil yawned, stupendously tired, but terrified of dropping back off. *Must stay awake.* He jumped back out of bed, threw on some warmer clothes and barricaded the door with a chair and a pile of revision books. *A zombie me will find it harder to get out now.* He knocked on the desk lamp and sat down, then slid out a diary which he had once written **VIRGIL** on in thick black sharpie. Recently, he had changed this to **VIRGILANTE.** He knelt at the desk and began to write:

Asda car park. Day five. Number of criminals brought to justice: 8. Patrols put on hold due to grounding.

His chest felt heavy, as if all the people he had punished were sitting on it. Gentle blue crept in through the dark curtains. He heard his mum moving about in bed. She had been making phone calls. Virgil was pretty sure she had arranged for Pastor Jerome to come and see him tomorrow. *Or is that today?* He sighed. 2:01 AM. *Today.*

She had also called his dad. Her words had been muffled, but by the way she was speaking, it was clear Tony was getting an earful. He shivered, closing the diary, then clambered into bed and buried his face in the pillow. He hated to think that he was the cause of another argument between his parents. He usually did everything he could to praise them to each other.

Lying on his side now, he watched the blinking red colon on his alarm clock. *I can't believe she caught me out.* Rows with his mum didn't happen very often, but when they did, boy did you know about it. She could be tenacious about discipline. There would be no loopholes, no relaxing the leash—if Mum said grounded, he was as good as handcuffed to the bungalow. *Unless I'm out sleepwalking. Imagine trying to explain that!*

A headline scrolled across his closed eyelids. He didn't want it to, but the words didn't care—2 AM was their favourite time to play.

HORROR CRASH ON THE A14.

Virgil knew the article off by heart. Certain phrases still haunted him:

'Trevor Lee, 38, had been drinking all morning when he got behind the wheel of his Ford transit.

Mr Lee took the corner at 90 miles an hour and on the wrong side of the road.

Despite the damage to his vehicle, Lee walked away with minor lacerations to his face and hands.

Mrs McAllister was left in the ditch while her new-born baby screamed in the backseat.'

Lee's face swam into focus. It was long and thin with hollow cheeks. Virgil knew his ugly mug from the paper.

From the tiny photograph he had traced with his finger. He knew it from the article he'd read by torchlight, under his bedsheets in the dead of night, hands trembling as the tears dripped off his nose. Virgil hated the people who had published it, making a quick buck from all their misery. He hated the sensationalism, the language, the way it gloried in the violence of the collision. He even hated the matter-of-fact way in which his mum's injuries had been described. Make a few jaws drop, keep people buying your newspaper, next story, next tragedy, move on, move on.

Virgil never had moved on, and Zelda couldn't. While Trevor Lee had lost his driving license and would be out of prison within ten months, the McAllisters had been forced to adapt to an entirely new way of life. Tony hadn't coped. He had thrown himself into his job as a social worker and neglected Zelda. Virgil hated this too, he hated how the tragedy had pushed his parents apart. Their house used to be full of the sound of reggae and raucous laughter.

As much as he loathed the newspapers, the focal point of all his resentment had always been Trevor Lee. Over time, he had managed to push Lee out of his day-to-day thoughts. Dwelling on him only poisoned things, leaving him unable to concentrate or even speak. Realising that the piece of filth was still ruining his life, even from prison, Virgil had vowed to stop brooding on him, and over time, his fantasies of torturing and killing the man had evaporated.

He slipped into an uneasy slumber. Then awoke with a start. His throat was hoarse.

From his mum's room, he heard, 'Virgil? Was that you?'

'Yeah, I think so.'

'Are you OK? Want me to come in?'

'Nah. Just a bad dream.'

'Sure?'

'I'm fine, go back to sleep.'

'OK, darling, as long as you're alright.'

'Fine, Mum.'

A pause.

'You're still grounded.'

'Night, Mum.'

'Night.'

CHAPTER TEN

SCONES

Virgil guided the bike over a patch of dry grass and pedalled furiously to get up speed, then sat straight-backed, flexing his fingers as the handlebars jittered precariously. He could not believe his luck.

At nine o'clock, Pastor Jerome had called to say he wouldn't be able to come to the house. Zelda had taken the call, the finger that twirled her hair indicative of the many cogs turning within. 'Could Virgil come to the Church?' Jerome had asked. His mum's initial response had been a curt, 'no.' But after five minutes of awkward silence, she had called the Pastor back and signed Virgil up for an hour of counselling—no more, no less. Zelda was taking Maisie to Birmingham to visit a friend and wouldn't be at home to enforce the grounding.

'You're to come straight back. Understood?'

'Got it.'

'No detours or pit stops, and if your chain comes off again, you're to call me first.'

'I know how to fix a chain now, Mum.'

'No excuses. I expect a call from this number,' she waggled the house phone, '11 AM on the dot.'

Steep street rolled on ahead of him in a never-ending incline. As his thighs felt the burn, Virgil reminded himself of the wind rush that awaited him on the journey back. If you started from St Justus, you could bomb down the hill and be at Stanley's Farm (the last property before the countryside) in one minute forty. He had timed himself; this was what you did when you had zero friends.

He resolved not to look at the crypt when he reached St Justus, just in case something was there. *Shudder.* Arriving at the gate, Virgil lifted his bike through and pushed it along the newly-laid path. Jerome had insisted they make the church more accessible for Zelda. A few older members made noises about the changes, but the old Pastor was having none of it. 'This church is the people, not the pavement!'

The Manse was at the far end of the graveyard, an ageing sandstone cottage with a thatched roof and faded green windows. Jerome lived alone; his wife had passed and their four sons had families of their own. Virgil made to go left around the church, which would avoid the crypt, but stopped himself. *I'm not going to let some stupid sleepwalking episode determine where I go.* He went right and dragged his eyes up to the vine-riddled doors. No one there. He propped the bike against a headstone and took his feet over to the sunken trapdoor. White creepers still covered the entrance. He tried both handles, giving them a good tug. They wouldn't budge. *Hmph, not so scary now.*

As he drew away from the crypt, Virgil noticed, as he had before, that the long grass underneath the cherry tree was flattened. *Shouldn't it have bounced back by now?* More puzzling was the fact that the rest of the grass was being tousled back and forth by the wind, but the levelled grass didn't even quiver. He was stood pondering this when he heard footsteps. His heart leapt right out of his chest. There was no pretending the sound had come from anywhere else. That was sole on stone. And it had come from behind the crypt doors.

'Is there someone down there?' Virgil squeaked. Nothing. 'Hello! Do you need help?' The wind was agitating. It moaned and whispered as it forged a path through the uneven gravestones, sending leaves spiralling skyward in ethereal columns. It bothered the collar on his jacket. Still, no one announced themselves from the tomb.

'I'll just be at the Vicar's. You bang on those doors if you need assistance!' Virgil didn't know what he was saying, but it was less scary to imagine he was talking to a person who'd locked themselves in, than to something that was trying to get out. He didn't turn his back on the crypt until he was a good fifty metres away. Closing the Manse gate carefully, he stole one last look, then parked his bike by Jerome's bench and rapped three times with the brass knocker.

Just being inside Jerome's walled garden made him feel safer. He used to love coming here. The Yeboahs had been close friends of his own grandparents. He had practically grown up in this garden. There was the stone crocodile which Gramps swore he and Jerome had caught, and the swinging seat, now overgrown with moss and looking very unsafe.

The door swung open and three cats escaped into the garden. Jerome had kept cats for as long as Virgil could remember. There was Luther—lean and black, Calvin—a Ginger Tom, and Zwingli—a beautiful tortoiseshell. Rumour was, they had been Mrs Yeboah's. Jerome stood in the doorway in an apron, with a tea-towel thrown over his shoulder.

'Virgil! So good to see you,' he held his arms wide, then let them drop. 'Sorry, I'd forgotten you didn't like that anymore,' he said in a growly voice, patting Virgil's shoulders. 'How's the face?' he turned Virgil's chin with leathery fingers, running concerned eyes over the bruising.

'Better actually,' Virgil shrugged off his jacket which Jerome took.

'Good to hear, brother. Come through, I've been baking for the fete this afternoon.'

Virgil followed Jerome to the kitchen in a daze. *The fete.* He had completely forgotten! Prestley's village fete was one of the highlights of the year. The freshly baked rolls, celebrated farm produce and big brass band had been a staple of his childhood. *What a day to be grounded!*

Jerome studied his fallen face. 'Yes. I got the impression Zelda didn't want you free-roaming. Don't worry,' he opened the oven, 'you can sample the goods before the other punters!' The Pastor lathered the scones with raspberry jam and placed a generous dollop of clotted cream on each one. 'Who cares if it's only ten o'clock?' he winked. 'When I was your age, I could eat cake from sunset to sunrise.' He busied himself by the sink, then came and sat down with two steaming mugs of tea. 'Talk to me.'

Jerome was an excellent listener. He placed his fingertips together just under his chin and watched with interest. He never interrupted, and only spoke occasionally to clarify a point or ask an insightful question. As he poured his heart out, Virgil began to feel comfortable. Ironically, it was the antithesis of the discomfort he often felt during Jerome's sermons. He left almost nothing out; the fight with Dauber and Pidge; his illicit Asda patrols. It felt good to share the weight of it all. The only information he withheld was Floyd's hat and the secret note. When he had finished, they sat in silence for a while. The cat flap went, it was Luther. The black feline purred and nuzzled something invisible by the pantry door. The Pastor walked to the bookshelf and came back with a Bible.

'Can I read you some scripture?'

'Sure.'

Jerome thumbed through the well-worn book, landing somewhere near the end. He cleared his throat.

'Do not avenge yourselves, beloved, but leave room for God's wrath. For it is written: "Vengeance is Mine; I will repay, says the Lord."' Jerome finished solemnly. 'Karma is a cruel master.' He closed the Bible. 'Everyone is crooked, depending on whose plumb line you're using. The real question is, who's lookin'? Is there an almighty judge up there, taking notes? Did he watch those boys beat you and tip your mother into the puddle with indifference? Or is he biding his time?'

The cat flap clacked—Zwingli the tortoiseshell. Virgil coaxed the moggy over. Jerome was right. Maybe all this madness would have to stop.

'We were grateful you were there in the car park, Pastor.'

'Right place at the right time. My walking stick's never seen so much action.'

'I'll think carefully about what you have said, I had better get out of your hair, thanks for the scones.'

Jerome held up a finger. 'Not so fast. There's one more thing.' Virgil scooched back into his chair, draining the dregs of his tea and trying to look composed. Zwingli hopped up and began kneading his thighs.

'Fire away.'

'I think you should visit them in hospital—those boys from the scuffle in the bathroom.' Virgil went to protest but Jerome held up a hand. 'Hear me out. When your friends return to school, they will be out for blood. There'll be a price on your head. Virgil, all this anger stored up inside of you—channel it in the wrong direction and it will change you, and not for the better. Take those boys a get-well-soon card, chocolates even. Bite your tongue, apologise if it seems appropriate. Do everything you can to establish *peace*, otherwise, when they return to full health, they'll get you, and they'll get you good.'

As Virgil was leaving, Jerome pushed a bag of scones into his hands. 'Give my love to your mum.'

'Will do. Thanks for these, wow they're still warm!' He waved as he popped the carrier bag over a handlebar and closed the gate.

'Oh, and, Virgil!' Jerome called after him, 'Don't go near that crypt! The doors are rotten, it's not safe!' Virgil shouted his agreement. *No problem, Pastor, I won't be going near those doors ever again.*

The ride home was one of his best times yet: one minute and twenty-four seconds. As he rounded the final corner onto Albion Street, Virgil felt cleansed; getting it all off his chest had been an incredible release. He was in time to call his mum too, with five minutes to spare. Suddenly, an afternoon indoors didn't seem so bad. There was bacon in the fridge. A crisp slice or two between some fresh bread, washed down with a glass of Maisie's strawberry milkshake. Things were looking up.

He skidded to a halt, sending gravel spraying onto Diane the snitch's petunias. There was a police car outside the bungalow.

CHAPTER ELEVEN

SPILT MILK

Virgil stowed his bike down the side, then let the officer in. Detective Inspector Anwaar Kaplan was a small Indian lady in her thirties. She had large brown eyes and her hair was tied up into a neat bun. She smelled of cinnamon. Virgil found himself utterly captivated, and had he not been so terrified of the charges about to be levelled against him, he might have enjoyed the meeting.

He ran the cold tap and poured himself a glass.

'Can I get you a d-drink?'

'No, thanks, I've got coffee in the car. I won't stay long.' *Sounds promising.* Virgil hopped onto the kitchen worktop.

'You going to get that?' Kaplan raised a thick eyebrow at the gushing tap.

'Oops, yeah, sorry.' He flicked it off.

'I've come with news,' she pulled out an iPad. 'We followed up a lead on the men from the assault.' If Virgil's jaw could have hanged any lower, it would have been touching his belt. Kaplan waited briefly for a response, then continued. 'We pulled CCTV from a traffic camera on the A7. It shows a blue Citroen Saxo driving in excess of one hundred miles per hour down the Oldley bypass. The footage was taken within minutes of the assault, so we put out an ANPR.'

'ANP what?' Virgil found his voice.

'It lets us know if the car pops up anywhere in the country. If the plate gets caught by any of our cameras, ANPR flags it and we move in. Anyway, turns out it wasn't necessary—the car was registered to a local address.' Seeing Virgil's expression, she quickly added, 'I can't tell you where. But it was an older gentleman. The car wasn't there, but under questioning, he admitted to his grandson driving a blue Saxo. I can't reveal the name to you.'

'In case I go and duff him up?' Virgil said drily.

Kaplan flashed him a dazzling set of teeth, 'It's protocol. But yes, it negates the risk of retribution.'

'So, did you find the guy? What happened?'

'We caught up with him at his girlfriend's flat.'

'And?'

'Well, now we have to find the others. I can't tell you much more than that, I'm afraid.' Kaplan made an awkward face, 'I know it's not what you want to hear. But there was no CCTV from the store, and our witnesses fell through.'

'What about me? I'm a witness.'

'Yes, and no doubt they will use your statement when it comes to trial.'

'And when will that be?'

'Maybe next April?'

'Next year?' Virgil blew long and hard. 'The driver filmed it all on his phone, nothing's surfaced online?'

'Not yet.' Kaplan's eyebrows pulled together in sympathy. 'The driver has a record, but there's not much on known associates and he's given no comment interviews. I'm sorry I couldn't come with better news. Is your mum back today?'

'Yeah, about seven.'

'How is she? I saw the pictures of her fingers.' Kaplan grimaced. 'Pretty horrible for her.'

'Mum's tough.' Virgil explained, 'I think it shook her up a bit though.'

'Do pass on my regards. I will try and visit again soon. Could you relay to her everything I have just told you? I left her a voicemail.'

'Yes.' Virgil was still waiting for Kaplan to cuff him for the spate of tyre-slashings. He didn't relax properly until he had watched her pull off.

He ate his bacon sandwiches while sketching in the back of the VIRGILANTE diary and daydreamed of DI Kaplan shining the V signal into the moody skies. She swooned as he swept in from the shadows, embroiled in dry-ice. *The Virgilante strikes again!*

He felt torn drawing mask designs and even a little guilty—Jerome had talked a lot of sense this morning, maybe he *should* ditch the diary. *What would I even do to a criminal? Give him a Chinese burn?* Virgil put the felt tips down. This was all a ludicrous pipe dream. Tomorrow morning, he would ask his mum to drop him at the hospital, *make peace*. He tapped a pen against his glass; a mouthful of milkshake left. He really couldn't be bothered to go make another. *Maybe I'll just finish this design…*

The house phone went, he jumped and sent the drink flying. 'Oh snap!' Then he saw the clock: 11.30.

Crap, crap, crap, crap, crap, crap! 'Oh, hi, mum! How's Birmingham?'

One trillion apologies later, he was able to hold the phone to his ear without the risk of an eardrum bursting.

'Shame about the evidence,' said Zelda, 'DI Kaplan sounds nice though.'

'Yeah, she was good.'

'Do I detect a hint of infatuation?'

'No,' Virgil lied defensively. 'Anyway, the police are useless.'

'Keep your shorts on, Romeo. How did your meeting with Jerome go? Hold on… let me just… no, Maisie, don't—'

The line went quiet. Then Zelda's voice returned, she sounded tired. 'Sorry, darling, I've got to go. Be good. We will be home around seven.'

Virgil got to cleaning up his desk. The milk had run all the way down the legs and soaked into the carpet. *Typical.* He scrunched up his ruined drawing. As he traced the milkshake's runny course, Virgil moved a box left over from Gramps' house. They had cleared it out when he died, and what couldn't fit in the McAllisters' loft had been squirrelled away all over the bungalow. With a dull stab, Virgil realised he had never looked in this box before. He slid his finger under the brown tape and lifted the flaps. Nestled in newspaper at the top of the box was a mask.

Wow, does this bring back some memories. The mask, with its curled horns and dead eyes, had always terrified Virgil and his cousins. A Ram. They had found it in Gramps' study and had been taking it in turns wearing the thing and chasing each other around the house when he caught them. '*The Ram*', Gramps had explained with a mischievous wink, was a family heirloom, and granted magical powers to the wearer. Much to their squealing delight, Gramps had put the mask on himself and chased them until tea time. Virgil smiled at the memory. Happier times. He hadn't seen his cousins since the funeral.

The Ram. He had forgotten how strange it was. Was this it? Was old mutton chops the answer? Didn't Bruce Wayne become the thing that scared him the most? He slipped it over his face and turned to the mirror.

Imagining the looks of terror on the faces of the Saxo lads. Virgil stepped through the mirror, out of his bedroom and into their marijuana-smoke lounge. He choke-slammed Michael Peña through the glass table, scattering the drugs paraphernalia. The skinhead brothers were frozen on the sofa—Virgil sunk a throwing knife into one and kicked the other unconscious as he dropped his Xbox controller and reached for a handgun. The final foe was Skull Sleeves. He turned and made a break for it, shattering the French doors and haring down the garden path. But Virgil was faster. The Ram had given him god-like speed. He caught up with old Skully before the garden ended and upper-cut him over the back-fence, Tekken-style.

It didn't hurt to fantasize. The police were dragging their feet, he would never see those lads again, and if he did, he wouldn't be in a position to upper-cut anyone. Virgil slid the Ram into a drawer and went to get a cloth for the milk.

CHAPTER TWELVE

THE VISIT

It had been threatening rain all morning, and as Virgil stepped out of his mum's car, the first fat drops made circles on the pavement. Despite being dropped close to the hospital entrance, he was soaked by the time he reached the doors.

The receptionist's lips puckered as he dripped on her station. Virgil was about to ask where ward three was when a flash like a camera going off surprised them both. He and the woman stopped to stare out of the panoramic windows. The lightning was followed by a deep roll of thunder that went on and on.

'A portent of doom,' the receptionist quipped.

'More than you know.' Virgil placed the cards and chocolates on the top and tried to wipe the blotchy droplets off. He only succeeded in smudging the names. His school mates were in different buildings and were a

ten-minute walk apart. He would visit Ben Pidgeon on
ward three first, and if he survived that, Daniel Dauber on
ward sixteen. Visiting hours were two until four at Oldley
General. As he walked the stretching corridors, giving
himself a pep-talk, Virgil practiced his pained-expressions.
He even had an apology lined up—albeit, one that didn't
specifically place the blame on himself. He was prepared
to make peace, not pretend they were innocent.

Ward three. Hand on the door. Heart doing William
Tell Overture on acid. The bays were quiet, with relatives
and friends sat around bedsides, talking in low voices.
Some of the patients had large privacy curtains drawn
around them. With a cold twinge in his stomach, Virgil
spotted Pidge. He was staring at him from a bed by the
window at the end of a row. There was no one else there.
Phew. That's one awkward conversation avoided. Virgil
approached the schoolmate he had put in intensive care.
His mouth felt like he had swallowed the Sahara.

'Hi, Ben.'

Pidge just stared. Virgil couldn't work out if it was
anger or shock. He was getting ready to leave the card and
chocolates on the bed and make a run for it, when Pidge
held out his hand. Virgil drew closer, still unsure. Pidge
flexed his fingers in a gesture that said, 'Shake it, I'm
waiting.' Fully expecting to be pulled in and stabbed,

Virgil put his hand out. They shook. Pidge's grasp was weak.

'I can't believe you're here,' Pidge said in a faraway voice. 'Everybody said you wouldn't show.'

'To be honest, Ben, I was never planning on coming. But now that I'm here, I'm wondering why it took so long. I'm so sorry that you're in here. Stupid question I know, but how are you?'

'I'm fine,' Pidge smirked. 'Food's horrible but there's variety. Plus, I'm something of a minor-celebrity. The nurses call me Pencil-boy.' Virgil struggled to keep a straight face, but then he and Pidge were both laughing. It was probably the relief of it all, but he felt light-headed.

Pidge stopped quickly as the pain in his side kicked in. Virgil went and got them both some water, and soon, they were chatting away like old friends. Pidge was lonely. His family hadn't visited much, and Virgil was upset to see only a handful of cards on the windowsill, including a big one from school. It turned out that he and the big guy had lots in common—they had both grown up in Prestley and their school trajectory was identical. After discussing teachers they hated and girls they fancied, Pidge suddenly blurted, 'I've had a lot of time to think in here. About my choices. Who I hang out with—'

Virgil butted in, 'Ben, you really don't have to say anything.'

'No, I do. Because while I've been sat here thinking about it—that day when I tried to strangle you. We were in the wrong. That Joshua never did anything to us. All you were doing was sticking up for him.' Pidge looked like he was fighting tears. Virgil averted his gaze and watched a nurse drain someone's catheter into a cardboard basin, then carry it carefully out of sight. After a minute or two, Pidge regained the ability to speak, 'I called school you know. Told that idiot, Doyen, I was changing my story— that you and Joshua were telling the truth all along. Did he get in touch?'

'Not a word, mate. I'm excluded for three weeks.'

'Cor, what a moron. Mind you, three weeks off!'

'I know, right? It has been eventful so far!'

'Stabbed any more people with pencils?'

They both chuckled, Pidge more gingerly this time, his hand over the patch. Soon, an hour had passed, Virgil figured he had better get over to ward sixteen if he was going to have time with Dauber.

'Hey, before I go. Have you had any contact with Daniel? I'm going to visit him next.'

'I'd guessed,' Pidge nudged the second box of chocolates with his toes from under the thin cover, 'I've texted him once or twice. No reply.'

'And is that normal?' Virgil could imagine that Daniel Dauber wasn't exactly the texting back type.

'Yeah… ish, but then, I'd have expected him to reply at least once. What else is there to do when you're stuck in here?'

'True. How much longer are they keeping you?'

'Not long actually—they seem to think I could come home in three or four days, providing nothing else ruptures.'

'I'm so sorry.'

'Don't be. The way I see it—if you hadn't shanked me with that pencil, then you'd be six feet under and I'd be spending a lot longer than two weeks locked up.'

On his way to ward sixteen, Virgil was buoyant. Pastor Jerome's advice had been spot on; smoothing things over with Pidge had gone swimmingly. They had swapped phone numbers and even arranged to hang out when Pidge was discharged. He felt far less anxious about visiting Dauber. With the chocolates under one arm, he pushed through the swinging blue doors.

Ward sixteen had a clinical smell, but not the clean type. It smelled as if someone had tried to mask the stench of urine and infection with some particularly strong bleach, but all one's nostrils really got was a cocktail of all three. The ward was separated into several large rooms off a long corridor. Virgil began to pass them, looking each time at the whiteboard outside for the names of the patients within. The beds were filled mostly with old people, many of whom were asleep or sitting staring straight ahead. It was vacant expressions all around. His limited knowledge told him this must be neurology, maybe even a stroke ward?

Daniel Dauber, room ten. The Matron's sloping hand read. Virgil rounded the corner. There were six beds, one empty. Two of them contained sleeping shapes. At the end of one bed sat a man in his forties, rocking back and forth, while a nurse talked calmly. The bed next to Dauber's had an old lady in who smiled very sweetly but had lipstick drawn on in a Chelsea smile.

There was a woman sitting on a plastic chair talking to Daniel. It was Gloria Welham, Daniel's Aunt. She was Chair of the Governors at Bulwark and had undoubtedly championed his three-week exclusion. As she rose to greet him, recognition spasmed across her face, changing her neutral expression to one of utmost disgust. She withdrew her hand and backed away, standing in front of Dauber protectively as if she thought Virgil were here to pull the plug.

Virgil held out the card and chocolates, 'I won't stay long.'

'No,' she snatched them out of his hands, 'you won't.'

Dauber was sat up in bed. He wore a padded red helmet which his normally impeccably styled hair stuck out of at bizarre angles. There were deep rings around his eyes and a line of cannulas going into his left hand. His appearance shocked Virgil. He wasn't sure he wanted to see him like this. It was an intrusion. Daniel had done this to himself, yes. But it was easier to imagine him as the knuckle-dragging under-eighteens kickboxing champ he was. Not this sorry mess. Virgil had his apology lined up. It would be nothing short of a miracle if he could leave here having made peace with both schoolmates. But Pidge had given him hope.

He began to speak, but Dauber cut him off. With great difficulty, he pushed himself into a more upright position. His bloodshot eyes bore into Virgil's, communicating a loathing beyond words. Then, with his grip on the bed-rail shaking the entire mattress, he spoke in a staccato stutter.

'When… I'm… out… break… your… neck.'

CHAPTER THIRTEEN

BAIT

3.15 approached with stunning urgency. When it came, Virgil fought his way to the front of the dawdling queue, plonking himself down directly behind the bus driver.

'You're eager,' said the old-timer, taking his aviators off and lifting his cap to scratch a balding scalp. 'Schools out for the Summer, eh!'

Virgil didn't reply. He was coiled like a rattlesnake, back to the window, watching the door. Bulwarkers trudged past, sweaty, their bags dangling limply off their shoulders. He heard Dauber before he saw him. He was boasting about something that had happened in PE. It wasn't the usual slew of flowing profanity—he was obviously still on the speech therapist's books.

It had been three weeks since Virgil's hospital visit. In assembly today, Mr Doyen had called Daniel Dauber's recovery *nothing short of miraculous*. Virgil felt *disastrous* would have been a better choice of word.

Dauber stopped short as he came up the steps, catching sight of Virgil. After a momentary pause (in which nobody pushed him because they were all terrified), he continued down the aisle to the back seats. The bus pulled off and fields began to sail by, a patchwork of yellow rapeseed and rippling meadows. Virgil missed all of the sun-scorched beauty of their journey as his eyes were locked on the rear-view-mirror. He had made it this far— he wouldn't be caught out so close to the finish.

Art folder in hand, he breathed deeply, then, as the doors hissed open, he leapt from the top step and hit the pavement running. The sounds of the other alighting children faded in a matter of seconds. Still, he ran until his lungs screamed for mercy and his bag straps had chafed his shoulders to shreds. Albion Street came into view. He shot past the turning and took a sharp left down the cut-through. It made sense to be unpredictable—Dauber didn't know he used the back door.

Into the bungalow, door locked, bag and folder flung into the hall, then lounge curtains drawn and onto the sofa to lie in wait and watch. As he peered through a slight gap in the curtains, Virgil's breathing began to slow. His heart-rate spiked a couple of times when a neighbour slammed their door, or a cyclist came past, but then the street quietened down. Nothing happened for an age. About ten minutes after his mad dash, Lucy White ambled past, her hair was stuck to her forehead. *Feeling the heat.* Then some year eight boys. A few cars sped past, a white cat rubbed itself on the hot tarmac for a while, but there was no sign of Dauber or anyone else. Virgil began to relax. It would be an hour and a half before his mum and Maisie were home.

He went to the fridge. They were well-stocked for strawberry milkshake mix but was there any milk? *Booya.* A four-pinter sat in the open door. Virgil had made himself a tall glass and was rummaging around the cupboards for some Jaffa cakes when a strange sound made him stop and prick up his ears. It was a high-pitched wheedling like an animal caught in a trap or a distant engine that came and went. As the sound got closer, he realised that it was a boy's voice, screaming and pleading. The pitiful sound was bolstered by the dissonant braying of many others, who screeched and jeered as they chanted, 'WEDGIE, VEGGIE, WEDGIE, VEGGIE!'

Virgil dropped the biscuits and rushed into the lounge. Being careful not to disturb the curtains, he inched forward and squinted through the crack. Immediately, a tall shadow lurched in front of the window. His hands were over his brow, trying to see in. Virgil threw himself onto the carpet and lay motionless at the foot of the sofa.

'Come out, Virgil! There's a friend here to see you!' It was the voice of Keegan Rice. His shadow turned back to look at the crowd, then bashed on the glass so hard Virgil thought it might shatter. He would have been quite content to stay put, lying under the sofa until they got bored and went away. But then the awful pleading started up again, and so did the chanting. 'WEDGIE, VEGGIE, WEDGIE, VEGGIE!'

Staying low, he crawled on his stomach into the hall. He tentatively pushed his fingers through the letterbox, opening it just wide enough to see out. A crowd of Bulwark students were gathered in the street opposite the bungalow. There were one or two girls amongst them, but it was mostly lads. Some of the rabble had taken their shirts off and tied them around their faces. Their school-ties were fastened around their heads like bandanas. Three or four bikes orbited the crowd. As the bodies shifted, Virgil glimpsed Dauber, he had tied his shirt around his waist and was wearing an actual balaclava. *He must have brought it to school.* He was grunting and lifting something. The higher he lifted it, the more insistent the pleading became. Then Dauber did a 180 and Virgil saw the object of their derision. In Dauber's meaty fist hung the stretched white fabric of a pair of boxer shorts. Joshua Brown dangled, his head drenched with sweat, his hands scraped raw by the unforgiving pavement.

As Dauber lifted again and the crowd resumed their chanting, Virgil got to his feet. He could see their shapes through the mottled glass. His hands bunched themselves into rocks and his whole body began to shake. He had never felt such a boiling fury. The only thing stopping him from opening the door was the image of his own body on the front lawn with his neck broken by Dauber, a grisly find for his mum and Maisie.

'Come on, Virgil! Joshua's got himself into a bit of a tight spot out here!'

'He needs some help pulling up his tightie-whities!'

'Come on out and wedgie the veggie!'

'Feeling *down* there, Joshua? This should give you a lift!'

The screaming. The pleading.

Virgil flung open the front door.

CHAPTER FOURTEEN
FIGHT OR FLIGHT

The crowd froze with Virgil standing in the doorway. Only Dauber moved, lifting his squealing victim higher than ever before dropping him awkwardly. Joshua lay still for a moment, his white boxers sticking up out of his trousers like the arches of a miniature McDonald's. Then he scrambled to his feet and ran. No one followed him. He got to his front door, scratched the key around the lock, and made it inside. *Thank goodness, now stay inside, Joshua, whatever you do, stay inside.*

'You got lucky last time, you whiny little Rasta!' Dauber's deep voice carried down Albion Street, reverberating off the red brick houses. 'Come on then! Come and… try again! What're you… waiting for?'

Using the architraves as starting blocks, Virgil pushed off. He ran full-tilt onto the road towards the gang. No sound escaped his lips. He saved that energy, channelling it through his arms and torso instead. He ran as if he were competing in the one-hundred metres, as if there was nothing in his way. Those nearest scattered, stepping back and even leaping out of the way. Only Dauber stayed put. Perhaps he thought Virgil would pull up short. But he didn't.

At the last second, he lowered his head like a bull and dropped his right shoulder, ramming it into Dauber's exposed side. The two of them went down together. Virgil hit the road hard—his face just inches from the kerb. Dauber let out a noise that suggested he had caught something tender. Virgil hoped he had cracked ribs, both old and new, he was so incensed at them all. Fancy picking on kind, careful Joshua, who had never said a bad word to any of them.

Being the first to his feet. He kept his eyes locked on Dauber. Slurred speech or not, the olive-skinned bruiser was still a kickboxing champ. Virgil had seen him fight before, his hands were wickedly fast, and because of his size, he towered over everyone in their year. Virgil took two measured steps backward.

Unbeknownst to him, Keegan Rice had sneaked up from behind. He grappled Virgil and succeeded in pinning both arms behind his back. In a moment of panic, Virgil almost lost his focus, *if Keegan keeps holding me like this, I'm a walking punch-bag.* He dropped to his knees, jolting them both. Feeling breath on the back of his neck, he jerked back in a whiplash motion, cracking Keegan's teeth on the top of his head. The impact sent squiggling white worms cartwheeling all over Virgil's vision. And for a frightening second, he blacked out completely. Then, with a monumental effort, he clawed his way back to consciousness and about-turned to face Dauber.

From the soft moans behind him, he could tell Keegan was badly hurt. The crown of his own head felt as though it had been pick-axed, but the biggest threat still lay ahead. Dauber was getting to his feet, puffing heavily as he prodded his ribs. Then he seemed to swallow the pain and brought his mallet-fists up, turning his body side-on and adjusting his feet into southpaw. *Oh, crud.* Virgil suddenly felt exposed. He had felled Dauber with the element of surprise still firmly on his side. Now he had lost that ally, the fight would come down to pure technique. Technique that he didn't have. It was fledgling versus falcon.

Dauber feigned left and span, roundhouse-kicking the air in front of Virgil's face. He could never have blocked it. The only thing that had saved him was Dauber's misjudgement. But before he could react, Dauber came in again with two jabs to his side. They landed almost painlessly, but as they circled each other in the crowded street, Virgil's insides started to sting like they had been brushed with nettles. As Dauber ducked and weaved, a wry smile played on his lips, replacing the snarl. *He knows this is already over.* Virgil tried to look unfazed, but the sky swirled like he was circling the plughole and the roofs and houses became a merry-go-round of blurred colour. Dauber swung in again and Virgil ducked it. And again—he pulled back in the nick of time, rough knuckles grazing his throat. *How long can I keep this up?* He wasn't thinking straight, the adrenaline seemed to have evaporated in the merciless sun. His arms ached even as he held them up, and his knees had gone to mush. It was like an out-of-body experience, or at least he wished it were, the pain from where the punches had landed seemed to penetrate to his internal organs.

There were two escape options: the bungalow's front door stood wide open, or a silver mountain bike ditched by one of the lynch mob. He began to take steps towards the bungalow, eyes always on Dauber, then, in his periphery, something moved near the house. Virgil threw it the briefest of glances. Carl Vance leant on the door, pinning it open. *There's no way I'm making it back inside without a following. Got to make tracks, lead them away from my mum and Maisie.*

Just then, Pam and Mick pootled around the corner in their little Peugeot. The engine sputtered to a stop as Mick braked for the line of Bulwark shirts. He waited for them to scarper. Mick was a patient man. Three students stood in his way. When it seemed clear that they weren't moving, he gave a short blast on the horn. The middle of the masked chumps made a rude gesture back. From the blonde hair and builder's bum, Virgil guessed it to be Sid Brethren. Everyone watched the car to see how the moustachioed milkman would react. Mick gave Sid and his wingmen a thunderous look and revved the engine. Then, when they still didn't budge, he reached for the car door.

Virgil switched his attention to Dauber—whose head had turned with the others, his furrowed mono-brow glued to the Peugeot. *This is my only chance!* Scurrying over to the abandoned bike, he grasped both handles and lifted, then ran almost the remaining length of Albion Street before mounting. The saddle was a little high, obviously set for someone with longer legs, but Virgil stood up and pedalled furiously.

'OI! OI! HE'S GETTING AWAY!' the angry voices rose up then dropped off, replaced by the echoing tap of many feet. Virgil made a left at the end of Albion, then let the wheels spin as he glided over the gravelly wasteland that fed into Cort Crescent. Deciding to risk it, he slalomed the bollards that guarded the entrance to dog poo alley. It wasn't the most direct route to his destination, but he stood more chance of losing Dauber this way. The familiar smell of Milkybar and fence paint filled his nostrils as he zipped between row upon row of back gardens. In the confines of the alleyway, the bike sounded like an angry wasp.

The blind bend came into view, Virgil prayed that there would be no one coming the other way. He was approaching it too fast to stop now anyway. He pulled the back brake and slid the back tyre around the hairpin. The alley lay empty. At the end of the leaf-dappled tunnel, Steep Street glimmered gold. The pedals locked tight, the chain engaged and he was off. Speed was the priority here, but he still made tiny adjustments to the handlebars, avoiding anything brown and piled. Just as he neared the end of the shortcut, a scrape of skidding tyres told him his hunters had hit the hairpin.

Virgil shot out of the alley and into the glare of the low afternoon sun. Pulling onto the road alongside a startled jogger, he began to pedal like mad. Both hands clung sweatily to the treacherous rubber handles. He put his head down and bit his bottom lip, pushing past the fire in his thighs and calves. The yellow line that paralleled the pavement snaked left, then right, then steady as he found his rhythm. He cycled like the bike-thief he was, trying to get up as much speed as possible before the twenty-two-degree gradient of Steep Street forced him into a familiar crawl. He changed up the gears. The whirr of enemy wheels was closer all the time, but he dared not look back.

The bus-shelter outside the Funeral Parlour gave him a glimpse of his pursuers; Dauber, Rice and Adam Dyke were hot on his tail, their legs also pumping like pistons. The scrubbed metal of the bus-shelter distorted their angry faces even further: three gargoyles on bikes.

A few hundred metres later, a wing mirror revealed that Dyke (who was on a BMX) had started to lag behind, his smaller wheels eating up twice as much tarmac as the bigger bikes Dauber and Rice rode. Virgil didn't let up, he mounted the pavement outside Dinah's tearoom to avoid a man walking his Dalmatian in the road, and was nearly upended when two mums pushing prams came out of the florists. *Nearly at the top.*

He was heading to the only place he thought he might be safe: St Justus. The church spire rose above the treeline like a great pale sword. The sky behind it was Aegean blue, cloudless and bare. Only another hundred metres and he would be at the churchyard. The unfettered sun lashed his back. A bead of sweat trembled at the tip of his nose and he brushed it away. It would be quicker to ditch the bike at the gate and make a break for it on foot.

It might slow them down. The church was always open, and Virgil could think of three or four hiding places inside where he would be undetectable to his unchurched assailants. He nudged the front wheel through the gate and wedged a handlebar between its wooden slats. Entrance blocked. Then he vaulted the wall, scraping his knee on an upturned piece of slate. Landing with a roll, he bolted across the grass, gaining speed as he hit the flagstones. Cries of frustration rang out across the churchyard. Virgil allowed himself a victory smile, his hand was already on the iron ring that worked the latch.

He looked back to see Keegan Rice pulling at the silver bike while Dauber waited. *So long, suckers.* He went to wrench the door open. It remained shut.

CHAPTER FIFTEEN

TRAPPED

Locked? St Justus was never locked during the day! Virgil rattled both handles, tugging at them with the little strength he had left. They remained silent and still. His mind raced. *The side door.* Sometimes Jerome used the side door after communion to get out without being accosted. He tore himself away from the main doors and powered down the East transept. *No!* The side door was locked too. Last chance, the Manse, he would have to call on Jerome. The final stretch of graveyard seemed to elongate as Virgil, dizzy with the exertion of Steep Street, pushed off from the cold stone and stumbled in the direction of the Manse.

Heavy thuds behind him heralded the arrival of Dauber and Rice. In a last-ditch attempt to save himself, Virgil yelled, 'HELP ME!' Then Adam Dyke, who had skirted the church from the opposite side, skidded his BMX to a halt ahead of him, blocking off the path. Before

Virgil could cry out again, a splintering blow caught him between the shoulder blades. He pitched forward. The path came up to meet him like a stone mattress. He rolled onto his back and caught Dauber's foot between his hands as it came stamping down. Dauber pulled off the balaclava and threw it aside. It landed on a gravestone where it hung—an empty face, soullessly watching the proceedings. Dauber folded his hands and leaned on his knee, pressing down so hard that Virgil felt his chest would implode. Dauber was shaking. A row of misshapen teeth jutted out from his bottom lip, and either side, white spittle foamed from the pink cave of his mouth. His dark eyes were wide with triumph; one was so red he must have burst a blood vessel during the chase. Dauber lifted off, then sat down on Virgil with a grunt, pinning his arms to his sides. Then he reached into his back pocket. What he brought out made every ounce of resistance drain from Virgil. Dauber unsheathed the four-inch blade, cruel notches from the grip drove up into a jagged tip. As he tossed it from hand to hand, the thin slice of metal almost seemed to disappear.

'Daniel, please,' Virgil whimpered.

'It's DJ to you, you piece of filth,' Dauber whispered. 'Maybe I'll carve it into your thick African skull so you remember it better.'

'DJ, Deej, I'm sorry. I'm so sorry. Please don't, please. I never wanted to fight. I don't want to fight now. I just want to go home.'

'You're not going home without something to show for it.' Dauber traced the knife along Virgil's cheek, it was surprisingly cold.

'Dddddo it on my body then, just cut m-m-my arm or my chest. Please don't cut my face.'

'Nah, cut his fayth. Carve ittup like a bitta jerk chicken!' Keegan Rice leaned over them, flapping his elbows and clucking. Keegan's whole chin was stained red. By the way he was speaking, Virgil guessed his head butt had dislodged a few teeth. The blood had dribbled down over Keegan's gelatinous body, making him look like some hideous man-child vampire. Adam Dyke appeared over Dauber's other shoulder. He looked less certain.

'Honestly, I wouldn't, Deej. Not that I'm telling you what to do or 'owt, but you could do time for that kind of thing. If you cut him like. GHB or summat, innit. The police are cracking down on knives and that. I wouldn't cut him, not worth it. Just knock him out then we can all go get an ice cream.'

It was at this point that Virgil's bladder released. His pants soaked up the most of it, but his bottom felt warm and wet against the hard path. Dauber sat on his chest fingering the knife. Eventually, he turned to the others.

'Hold him.' Dyke and Rice obeyed, each one taking an arm and pinning a leg with their own knees.

'Aw, what? He's wet himself!'

'Disgusting.'

Dauber went about searching pockets. He pulled out Virgil's phone—an old Samsung with a heavily scratched screen—his only way of contacting his mum. Then from the other side, his wallet. With a look of disappointment, he pocketed the debit card and coins. Then he slid out the only photograph Virgil kept on him. It was a polaroid of his mum throwing him up in the air as a toddler, back when she could walk. Virgil liked to look at it sometimes. He knew what was coming, still, he begged Dauber.

In a small voice, he said, 'Please don't.' Then smaller still, 'Daniel, if it was your mum you'd understand, wouldn't you?'

Dauber flew into a rage. He rushed at Virgil and screamed into his face, spit flying, 'DON'T YOU DARE TALK TO ME ABOUT MY MUM, YOU WASTE OF SKIN! MY MUM IS DEAD!' The word rang off the headstones in shrill little fragments. Dauber stood again, his chest heaving as he regained some composure. Then, with a callous smile, he tore the polaroid into pieces and held them on his palm, blowing them into the wind.

Keegan was obviously tiring. He wobbled a loose tooth with his tongue.

'So, are you gonna slithe him up or what?' Dauber seemed to be ignoring his friend. He was looking around the graveyard. Keegan stood up, 'DJ! Hey! DJ! Are we cutting him or what?' Dauber sauntered back over, a look of delight plastered across his brutish features.

'Get him up and follow me.'

As his two lackeys dragged their victim along, Dauber hummed a tuneless dirge. Virgil let his tired feet drop as they hoisted him over the uneven grass and mossy stones. Only when it was too late did he realise Dauber's intentions.

He struggled against Dyke and Rice, but they held him easily while Dauber began to tear at the crypt doors. The vines came away in little puffs of powder that coated his sweat-drenched body in a weird paste. Eventually, he had removed enough creeper to get at the handles. Rice held Virgil alone, while Dyke helped pull one of the thick doors open. It gave an enormous creak that sent ice waterfalls down Virgil's spine. It was all one big nightmare. There was no waking up this time either. No running home. He stared into the gaping maw. Then all three of them had their hands on him, he struggled and kicked and shrieked and thrashed, but they walked him solemnly up to the dark opening and shoved him in.

Virgil tumbled down a flight of almost-vertical steps. All the breath was knocked out of him as he lay on his back and watched his three schoolmates work on the door. It screeched even louder on its way shut and plunged him into pitch blackness with a dreadful thud. He willed himself upward, but fell back exhausted, and listened as the conspirators discussed their next move.

'With any luck, no one will think to check in there.'

'Yeah, he'll have to eat rats to survive.'

'Here, come and help me with this.'

Virgil knew instantly what they were doing. To the side of the church lay some old railway sleepers, leftover from the bell-tower renovation. He lay and listened as they grunted and staggered their way over to the crypt. They repeated the journey twice, each time wedging a sizeable chunk of wood against the trapdoors. With every quivering crash, bits of earth and dust showered him. Until it all went quiet. The sounds of their voices died away and he was left alone in the damp.

Unlimited power lives within the crypt.

He could feel the panic rising. The hairs on the back of his neck stretched out like antennae, straining for signs of movement in the cold tomb. Virgil couldn't bring himself to turn around. What if it was right behind him? Employing some strange childhood logic, he squeezed his eyes shut and raised himself gingerly to his feet, turning as he did so. Anxious not to make any kind of noise that would disturb whatever slept down there, he shuffled back up the earthy steps until his head touched the barricaded doors. His eyes were still scrunched shut. *I've got to open them soon. Otherwise, I'll never find a way out. I'll be just another dead guy amongst… dead guys.*

There was only one thing for it. *One… two… three…* Virgil forced his eyes open. He had to bite his fist to keep the scream from leaping out.

There, in the darkness, something stared back.

CHAPTER SIXTEEN

THE SIX SAINTS

Virgil crouched, facing his mysterious watcher. After one whole agonising minute, the eyes blinked lazily and vanished.

'Hello?' His voice rang hollow from the clammy walls. 'My name is Virgil McAllister. I'm very sorry to have disturbed you. Hello?'

Something brushed against his shins. He drew back, falling onto his bottom with a wet splat. The darkness ahead of him was empty, but there was a sound like a pint-sized petrol engine that came and went. A furry flank brushed past again, then something nuzzled his hand and a rough tongue began to lick his fingers. Virgil suddenly felt very foolish. 'Zwingli? Is that you?' The cat purred louder, winding herself affectionately between his legs. Then she jumped up and began to knead his lap. Ten little needles punctured his thighs as she padded. Virgil let

Zwingli get comfortable, after the hellish day he had endured, it was nice to feel the warmth of another creature. He stroked the tortoiseshell coat. As his senses gradually adjusted to the darkness, he was able to make out the pattern. Zwingli purred her pleasure; her almond eyes became slits. Once or twice, a noise out of Virgil's range of hearing made them widen. When this happened, the tiniest shaft of light from the obstructed doors refracted the light, giving Virgil an up-close view of her opalescent orbs. *Cat's eyes. Of course! I am a certifiable dummy.* 'It was you gawking back at me the other night.' He scratched behind her paper-thin ears.

A thought crossed Virgil's mind that he immediately tried to banish. *If it was Zwingli who gave me such a fright on Sunday night, who opened the crypt doors? Or did I dream that bit? One minute they were wide open, and the next…* The stone tunnel waited expectantly. Virgil shooed the cat off his lap, turned to the freshly blocked doors and pressed his hands against them. He shoved with all his might. They lifted slightly, but not enough. The worn steps were smooth and prevented him from getting any purchase with his equally worn school shoes. The sleepers held.

There was nothing for it. Unless he wanted to spend the night down there—and boy did he not—he was going to have to search for an alternative exit. He stooped to scratch Zwingli's back. 'You managed to get in here

without the trapdoors. Fancy showing me your secret?'
She mewed and sauntered off down the dingy passage.
Virgil followed. His wet trousers clung horribly to his
buttocks. It was cold down here. Away from the surface, it
was hard to imagine the thirty-degree heat that besieged
Prestley.

The steps went down at a gentle angle that quickly
evened out. They came to a rectangular room. Shelves cut
into the walls suggested where the bodies would once have
lain. Virgil was relieved to see no ex-parishioners in the
gaps. Was this it? This tiny tomb? For such a grand set of
doors, he had expected more. Zwingli had disappeared.
He soon found her rolling on one of the stone shelves.
Then she transformed, suddenly alert. She looked to the
back wall as if a family of mice was tap-dancing along it.
Virgil came down next to her and ran his hand along the
chiselled rock.

There was a sound like a millstone rolling and Virgil
fell away from the shelf with a cry. The back wall had slid
away. 'Indiana Jones style,' he whispered. He crawled to
peer through the gap. There was nothing moving in there
except for Zwingli, who had already hopped through and
was chasing some invisible prey. Virgil stood back, hands
on hips. In most horror films, crawling through the egress
would be considered suicide. What choice did he have
though? It was the only way out.

He emerged into a chamber with a domed ceiling. A pinprick of light pierced the gloom from the dome's dead centre, it was the only source of illumination. Virgil was surprised at how high the ceiling went, he and Zwingli must be deep in the hillside. Stationed around the room in secluded recesses were six statues. Each assumed a unique pose. *Weird.* Carved in white stone, the statues all had one aspect of their outfit highlighted in gold-leaf. There were three women and three men. The women's golden items were a belt, a breastplate and a dagger. The men had a helmet, a shield and some shoes. It did not escape Virgil's notice that the golden shoes had winged heels. *Like the stained-glass dude at church.* He walked around the outside of the room squinting up at their noble faces, the craftsmanship of the sculptures was not unlike Michelangelo. The six sentinels stood on pillared bases, a raised tablet set proudly under each one's feet revealed their names: ST YOLANDE, ST BEATRICE, ST INGRID, ST FELIX, ST LUDAN, ST CLAVIUS.

In line with the statues and arranged in a ring that encircled the pin-prick of light were six stone sarcophagi. Each tomb was jet black, highly polished, and with streaks of pearl running through the marble. They were topped with an effigy of their corresponding saint. Six sets of eyelids closed in perpetual slumber, six hands pressed together in prayer, six pairs of feet which met in the middle. As Virgil paced the solemn circle, he noticed that a small carving of every golden accessory adorned the head of each sarcophagus.

Unlimited power lives within the crypt. He shivered. *Well, this is creepy.* 'Come on, Zwingli, time to try one of these other passages.'

Zwingli completely ignored the summons; she was sat on her haunches atop the feet of St Beatrice, clawing at the dust which swam in the 13th-century spotlight. Virgil sighed. 'Cats.'

There were two archways. He chose the closest. The passageway took him deeper and the floor was laid with the same stone slabs. Here and there, the weight of all the earth above them had collapsed the tunnel side or made the ceiling lower. He used his hands to feel the way ahead, and after a few metres, had to crawl as the shaft plateaued. Then, without warning, things opened up again and he was able to stand. The air seemed a fraction warmer, and if he was not mistaken, he could smell cooking. The smell grew stronger, then Virgil stubbed his toe on what proved to be the first in a narrow set of stairs that curved up and away in a spiral. He followed the staircase on his hands and knees. Music played from somewhere above, it was a Miles Davis record, he recognised it from Sunday afternoons at Gramps' house. A bassy voice rasped along to the trumpet solo. *Pastor Jerome?*

Eventually, he came to a rough wooden door. It was half the size of a regular door, like something you might see on a garden playhouse. There was a sickle moon carved into the wood as a peephole. Virgil pressed his eye against it. All he could see were some old barrels and a stack of discarded pews. Did the Manse have a basement? He tried the handle: locked. Virgil wasn't sure why, but he didn't feel like shouting to Jerome for help. Was it because the Pastor had warned him away from the crypt? Would Jerome believe that Dauber had forced him inside? *I'm not calling for help just yet.*

He could hear Zwingli mewing somewhere behind him. Filled with fresh confidence, Virgil turned from the Manse's secret door and retraced his faltering steps.

CHAPTER SEVENTEEN

THE CAT AND THE COFFIN

Zwingli had left the sunbeam and was scratching at a sarcophagus lid. Virgil went over to see what she was fussing over. It was one of the men. He followed the line up to the coffin dweller's alabaster doppelganger: ST CLAVIUS. The towering figure stared down his aquiline nose at Virgil, who turned back to the cat. To the left of the sleeping saint's knees, there was a crack which had widened into an opening the size of a man's fist. It was into this hole that Zwingli clawed, her front leg was in up to the shoulder.

'Pssk!' Virgil scared her off and came alongside the tomb. Immediately, he was above the crack and something dazzled from within. Intrigued, he went to reach inside, then stopped. This was exactly the kind of rookie error they made in the movies. Instead of offering his fingers as a chew-toy for zombie St Clavius, *shudder,* Virgil put one sweaty palm on the head and the other on the hands of the recumbent saint and pushed. It was incredibly heavy, but after a few shoves, the lid came away, dust billowing up from inside as Virgil inhaled and spluttered. He leaned over the edge, half expecting to be jumped by a rotting corpse. Inside the marble box lay an assortment of bones, loosely in the shape of a person. In the top corner, a skull grinned lopsidedly, its mandible was unhinged by decades of decomposition. Even in the dank semi-darkness of the crypt, the forehead was startlingly white. Ribs poked haphazardly out of the shreds of what may have once been a tunic, and the leg bones were stacked at the bottom of the coffin like spare puzzle pieces. Over the rest of the torso lay a large shield—it was an odd diamond shape and perfectly matched the gold-leafed replica on the alabaster Saint Clavius who still glowered, now overlooking his own disinterment. Virgil brushed a thick layer of dust off the shield boss; a tiny **c** had been hammered into the metal. *Clavius. It all looks so dry and dead. Which bit glinted?* He tried to lift the shield and was shocked when the entire thing disintegrated in his hands, leaving him holding onto the rusted iron rim clamps. The boss landed with a clunk and rolled to be with its owner's foot bones. As the flakes settled, they revealed Clavius' arms, which were locked in an x around a length of golden chainmail. The glittering strap had once been attached to the shield. *Is it called a buckler?* Virgil's knowledge of medieval weaponry was sketchy at best. Even so, the golden shield grip baffled him. *Surely you would put the priciest bit on show, at the front of the shield.* He was about to try and prise the buckler from Clavius' bony fingers when he noticed Zwingli. The tortoiseshell stood rigidly, bottlebrush tail down. Her pupils had become dark pools and both ears swivelled like satellites. A second or two later, Virgil heard it too. There was someone coming down the third passageway. For a heartbeat, he copied the cat; frozen at the graveside like a seventh saint. The trapdoors were blocked and he didn't like the idea of scrambling through the Manse crawlspace. *Not with something scrambling after me.* He looked into the empty sockets of St Clavius.

'Sorry about this, Clav.'

Hoisting himself over the lip, Virgil stepped awkwardly into the sarcophagus. With the lid at waist height, he pulled it back as far as he could, then squeezed inside and lay amongst the bones. Using his feet, he managed to shift the lid so that it was all but closed, a tiny sliver of amber highlighted the edge. He lay and listened, Clavius' withered hands pressing into his back.

The steps came closer and closer. They were ungainly; one foot dragged. When they reached the crypt, they stopped. Virgil held his breath. Inside the stone coffin, the sounds of his own body were accentuated. His pulse throbbed in his eardrums, but he kept perfectly still, anxious not to rattle any parts of the skeletal saint. Zwingli mewed several times. As Virgil tried to slow his breathing, he was sure he could hear her purring. After a while, the steps receded. Virgil couldn't be sure, but he thought they had retreated up the same tunnel. *That's it, I'm out of here.* He pushed the lid open and moved to jump out. Something knocked against his leg. Virgil extricated one of Clavius' forearms from his belt, where it dangled by a finger. The gold caught his eye again. He sucked his gums as he brushed the glistening shield grip with his foot. It flopped over invitingly, revealing new patterns. *I'm no graverobber. But then,* he shrugged, *Clavius isn't using it himself. It could be worth something.* Crouching in the coffin, he picked the remaining fingers off the grip, then wrapped it around his forearm, tying it in a crude knot. It was strangely warm. *Probably from me lying on it.* Virgil pressed it to his lips, testing its temperature, then remembered he'd just wrenched it from the grip of a dead guy. *Ugh.* He spat, making Zwingli scarper. Seized by a sudden desire to leave, he hurried up the passage that led to the graveyard. He would give the trapdoors one last try. Then, last resort, return to Jerome's moon door and bang on it until he appeared. *I'll kick it down if I have to.*

The trapdoor remained impassable. Virgil tried focusing on just one of the doors. *If I can rock it a bit, the top sleepers might roll off.* He put his shoulder in, again and again. The door would lift ever so slightly up to a point, but the weight of the blockade proved too much. Between shoves, Virgil stopped and listened, straining his ears for the sound of anything coming up the tunnel, anything that dragged.

On a particularly hard push, something shifted. A sleeper rolled off with an earthy thud. The trapdoors quaked, their iron handles swinging. Then the screech of bending metal lashed the stone walls. Dirt and pebbles showered Virgil. He covered his eyes and tripped, startled by his success. Falling and landing several steps below the shuddering doors, squinting up as the blinding sunlight poured in.

Then the left door gave way. Ripping off its own hinges with an ear-shattering scream, it fell towards him. There was no time to move, no time to think. Virgil braced himself with a whimper.

CHAPTER EIGHTEEN

INVINCIBLE

The door bounced once, eclipsing the entrance as it flipped. There was a splintering impact. He felt the immense weight jolt through his forearms and down into his core. The ancient timbers clunked and thudded all around him as the debris came to an echoing rest. Then there was perfect stillness. He was surely dead— the largest part of the door had hit him head-on. But as Virgil opened his eyes, he saw sunlight again. Two panels of blackened wood lay either side of his quivering body. Over his bended knee there rested a thick sleeper, it was snapped into a triangle; jagged needles jutted out like crosshairs where the collision had forced it asunder. Virgil's shin sat snugly within the apex of the gap, almost as if the heavy beam had split over his kneecap. *What on earth?*

He sat up, too weak to push the ruined doors off, and wiggled backwards, slithering out of the boy-shaped crevice. How had he survived? He checked his hands, there was no bruising, they didn't even hurt. *Impossible.* Virgil tried to lift the portion of door that had smashed into his upturned palms. It wouldn't budge. The golden buckler on his forearm reflected the sun into his eyes. He rotated it, tracing the delicate markings. *Is this what saved me? Clavius' shield grip?* Eager to reach the surface, he clambered over the mangled hinges and made his way to freedom.

The air in the graveyard was heavy with a Summery nectar. Virgil drank it in, savouring every delicious lungful. He could still taste the dank recesses of the crypt at the back of his mouth. His vision swam, all the headstones shone like mirrors, and the miniature roofs of Prestley shimmered through a curtain of heat. For the first time in hours, Virgil realised that he was incredibly thirsty. *Home, I need to get home. Mum will be going spare.* What was the time? He couldn't even call her. *They took my phone. They took my wallet. They took…* He watched Dauber rip his mum into a hundred fluttering pieces again.

He fiddled with the shield grip. In the evening light, it was almost transparent. The metal was so thinly woven that it felt like silk. Could it be? Could it really be that the ancient souvenir had protected him from the falling door? *Unlimited power.* Virgil drew strength from the idea.

He unravelled his rolled-up shirt sleeve and buttoned it over the shield grip, then dittoed the other arm for symmetry. *No sense in showing off my new bling.* Glancing back at the crypt, Virgil saw that only one sleeper remained, precariously balanced on the door that hadn't caved. Upon leaving the church grounds, he found the silver bike propped against a boundary wall. Dauber, Rice and Dyke obviously hadn't returned it to its owner, so he hopped on and let Steep Street work its magic. He blazed down the hill, braking once for a pigeon and again for a bag of McDonald's which he carried to the nearest public bin. *Not the 'cleaning up the streets' I'd had in mind. Gotta start somewhere.*

Zelda's car was on the drive. Virgil ditched the silver bike not far from where he'd first taken it and walked up the front path. Before knocking, he slunk down the side of the bungalow and unwrapped the shield strap. Bunching it in one hand, he carefully let it down into his bedroom through the open window. Then he returned to the front and rapped three times.

His mum came to the door. 'Virgil! We've been worried sick!' Behind her, Pam and Mick waved from the kitchen table. 'Mick's been driving around the village looking for you. He told us what happened.' As Virgil bent for Zelda to hug him, she noticed his trousers. 'Oh, darling, you're sodden! Is that… is it? Oh, darling.'

Virgil's bottom lip wobbled. Then it all came tumbling out. A wretched torrent of salt. Messy. He cursed himself for it, this show of weakness, in front of the neighbours too. The story came out in garbled bursts as he fought for breath against a tide of tears. When he got to Dauber's knife, Pam's fingers went over her mouth, while Zelda checked all over his face for cuts. He told them all about being barricaded in the crypt. But left out everything between that and his escape. 'The doors just gave way.'

When he had regained control of his breathing, he turned to Pam and Mick, 'I'm so grateful you came home when you did.'

'So are we,' Mick's eyes crinkled sympathetically.

Pam rubbed her husband's broad shoulders. 'What those toe-rags didn't know, Virgil, is that Mick was in amateur boxing before he worked the milk rounds.'

'What happened?' Virgil's mouth widened, his misery forgotten.

Mick looked sheepish. 'When I got out of the car, they all surrounded me, shouting. So, I bosh, bosh,' he mimed two lightning jabs, 'and the rest reconsidered.'

'We called the police over an hour ago,' Zelda explained. 'They said it wasn't an emergency and to call when we found you.'

'Where's Maisie?'

'Asleep. I put her down as soon as we got back. Anyway, you go and get in the shower, just chuck your clothes on the wash basket and I'll sort them later. I'm going to call Tristan Dauber.'

Virgil didn't protest. In truth, he was too exhausted to argue. Best to let the adults run through the motions, do whatever protocol dictated. He thanked Pam and Mick again and apologised for ruining their afternoon. Then trudged down the landing, stripping off as he went. He flicked the shower on, then stole into his bedroom and picked the golden shield grip off the radiator. He took it with him. Locking the door, he wound it around his arm again and stepped under the refreshing spray.

Virgil washed his hair and ran soapy hands all over himself, checking for bruises. Aside from where Dauber had caught him, there were no new marks. Intrigued, he rifled through the cupboard for one of his mum's razors. Carefully extracting a blade from the plastic head, he held it at arm's length and navel gazed, deep in thought. *Am I going crazy? Or does this shield strap have mystical powers? Only one way to find out…* He struggled to pick a piece of skin to experiment on, but in the end, he went with his thigh. He placed the razor's edge against the skin, bit into his knuckle, and swiped. Nothing, no stinging pain, no slit that opened up and bled. He did it again, same result. The edge of the steel bit sharply, but its cutting power was non-existent. He moved onto his left bicep: nothing. Then his thumb: nothing. Just to be sure it wasn't blunt, he used the blade to carve a V into the soap. He let a laugh of amazement ring off the bathroom walls.

'You alright in there, lovely?' Zelda's voice at the door. *She's been listening in. Probably worried about me.*

'Absolutely fine. *Better than fine.* I'll be out in a sec.'

~ ~ ~

Teatime passed in a whirl of phone calls and toddler-flung mashed potato. Virgil listened red-faced as Zelda called around her friends until she had acquired Tristan Dauber's address and number. She went out of the room for this one, but her cross voice could be heard barking through the stud walls even as Maisie sang and giggled her way through pudding.

Zelda came back in with a face like an anvil. 'That man is as conceited as they come.' She crunched the phone back into its holder. 'He had the audacity to berate me!'

She put on a deep voice, '"My son's never been the same since yours ambushed him in the toilets. He can't speak properly, he can't do this, he can't do that."' She snorted furiously, 'Tristan's delinquent offspring is going around the village with a *knife*. And *I'm* expected to apologise!'

'What did you say?'

'I said they had spoiled Daniel rotten long before June got her diagnosis, and probably even more after she found out it was terminal. That poor boy has always been given whatever he wanted. I said that maybe if Tristan introduced some boundaries in Daniel's life, he wouldn't get his kicks hurting other children.'

'And?'

'He put the phone down at June's name,' Zelda smirked, she wheeled to the window and stared at the yellowing lawn. 'She was a wonderful woman, June Dauber. Exceptionally kind. In a way, that was their downfall; they loved little Daniel to Jupiter and back, but no amount of toys or expensive holidays can make up for losing your mother.'

'I love you, Mum.'

'And I love you.'

CHAPTER NINETEEN

NIGHT RAID

Virgil pretended to be asleep when his mum came in. He waited until things had gone quiet in her bedroom, then pulled on his darkest jeans, a scarf and a navy hoodie and crept down the landing, being careful to avoid the creaky floorboard. In the kitchen, he used one of Maisie's wax crayons to make a rubbing of the notepad Zelda had written the Daubers' address on. He held it against the moonlight:

18 Windermere Way,

Fleddley,

Derbyshire,

OL2 0GT

Perfect. Just before he left, he ducked into the cleaning cupboard and carefully extracted a pair of latex gloves. Closing and locking the back door as firmly as he dared, he got onto his bike and began the twenty-minute ride to Prestley's adjacent village. Before bed, his mum had been talking about paying the Daubers an early morning visit to retrieve the phone and wallet. There was absolutely no way Virgil would allow this, but Zelda would not be dissuaded. If he wanted to avoid a monumental showdown, he would have to get them back himself, tonight.

It was one in the morning. There were very few vehicles on the back road, and the ones that passed him did so generally without incident. One car that came barrelling around a hedgerow flashed frantically as it *VROOOMED* by. Then, as *Welcome to Fleddley,* glimmered up ahead, a van made him wobble like a jelly in a hurricane. When he got to the village, he whipped out his wax rubbing and double-checked the house number. Daniel and his dad had moved out of Prestley a year or two after June Dauber died. Virgil had never seen their new place. Still, he had a few hours while people slept, and Fleddley wasn't big. He could surely find the house before time ran out.

He ghosted the streets until a bunch of conifers cast their shadow over a sign: **Windermere Way**. He cruised down the middle of the street, clocking number eighteen but not stopping. Then, burying the bike in a hedge, he walked back, hood up and hands in his pockets. Number eighteen was detached, with a double garage and a long sloping drive. There were two BMWs parked facing the road.

Virgil pulled the scarf over his face, walked straight up the drive and tried the side gate. Bolted. *Hmph.* But as he gawped at the high fence, he realised that the neighbour's bins were positioned right next to it. Climbing gingerly onto the blue lid of the recycling bin, he swung himself over, dropping silently onto the Daubers' patio. *Like a ninja.*

He was sizing up a pane of glass in the back-door, when instinct made him try the handle. It was open. Virgil checked that Goldie (he had taken to calling her that) was securely fastened. The crypt souvenir coruscated in the pale starlight. He took off his trainers and tucked them behind a plant pot, then set his Casio stopwatch going and plunged into the dark house. *Five minutes, in and out.*

The blue of the Daubers' internet hub backlit their colossal TV. At the far end of the diner-come-lounge, an answerphone message blinked in accusatorial red. All the doors were open. Virgil glided through the kitchen and into the hall. There was no basket so far and he couldn't smell dog. *Funny, I'd always imagined Daniel to be a dog person.*

The staircase went up onto a square patch of carpet and then left, he padded upwards, being mindful not to touch the bannister. On the landing, there were five doors. Two were open. The first open door was clearly the bathroom—he could see the basin through the lucent crack. The second led to what appeared to be a study; hundreds of books lined the walls, along with a vast collection of films. Virgil leaned into this room, running jealous eyes over Dauber's gaming setup. *How many consoles does one imbecile need?*

It was time to start trying closed doors. He slipped on the latex gloves. In all the excitement, he had almost forgotten them. Of the three remaining bedrooms, one door had coat hangers over its handle, *too noisy.* One was plain, *Daniel's dad?* And one had a large poster of a girl in a bikini on it. *Daniel.* Hoping against hope that Mr Dauber Senior didn't have a penchant for swimwear models, Virgil creaked the brass handle—*woah, that needs some oil*—and opened it the slowest he had ever opened anything. When there was a gap wide enough for him to slink through, he did. Daniel Dauber lay, fully-clothed, across his bed. He wasn't even under the covers. A half-eaten bucket of KFC sat idly by, while the whole room was thrown into stark relief by the flashing TV in the corner. It was a late-night movie. The Hurt Locker, by the look of it. *Cracking film. Shame Tae Kwon Dope is asleep.*

He crept in further. There was a pervasive aroma of sweat, unsuccessfully masked by Lynx Africa. Virgil was pretty sure every boy their age had a room that smelled like this. He tiptoed over a spilled bowl of Wotsits and started to open desk drawers. *If I were an egotistical maniac, where would I hide a stolen phone and wallet?* He searched on. The deep rumble of Dauber's breathing gave the mission a comforting ambience. Every few minutes, he would stop abruptly, mid-snore and have a scratch, or smack his lips. At these junctures, Virgil would pause and check the bed, making sure his arch-enemy was still horizontal. The sleeping grunt even mumbled his name at one point, that *really* got the blood pumping.

Virgil looked at his watch; seven minutes. He was getting close to bottling it and leaving, but the thought of his mum screaming her head off at Tristan Dauber kept him going. *I've got to find that phone.* Hands trembling, he leaned over Dauber's flattened form and slipped a hand into his pocket. There was nothing there but lint and a packet of cigarettes. He kept the fags. *Dirty habit, Deej.* Then turned and saw Dauber's balaclava and jacket hanging on the back of the door. *The one place I haven't looked!*

Virgil could have screamed. His phone and wallet were in the first pocket he checked. He shook his head, smiling. There had been no need to scour the whole room.

Worst. Burglar. Ever. He stowed the items he had come for, then reached into the other pocket and drew out the serrated knife. A phrase came into his head. *An eye for an eye and a tooth for a tooth.* He looked around the desk for something he could take. His gaze lingered on a kickboxing trophy before settling on a photograph of Dauber's mum. Virgil's cheeks burned and his neck prickled—he pocketed June Dauber quickly. Then he picked up a permanent marker and scrawled a message on the TV screen: **Next time, I won't miss**.

He flipped the knife in his hand. Walked over to the bed, and sank it deep into the pillow next to Dauber's face. Then exited the room quickly, down the stairs, through the hall and kitchen, only stopping when he reached the starlit patio, panting, but grinning from ear to ear.

He grabbed his trainers from behind the plant pot and was slipping them on when he saw the dog. A huge Alsatian crawled towards him from the kennel—*the kennel!*—at the end of the garden. It was giving off a low growl, its shiny black lips pulled back over gritted incisors. Its head was down, its tail between its legs. Virgil inched to his feet, *nice doggy*, not daring to look at the gate. *Nice doggy, nice doggy, nice—*

The Alsatian barked once then started to run.

CHAPTER TWENTY

KRAV MAGA

The dog was on him in a flash. Its jaws closed around his wrist and Virgil flinched, expecting searing pain, but instead, there was a crunch, and the animal yowled, backing off and whimpering. Virgil checked his skin. It was immaculate—no puncture wounds to speak of. He kissed the ancient shield strap. *Goldie, you beauty!* As he got to his feet, fragments of broken dog teeth skittered onto the slabs.

'Sorry, girl,' he felt a stab of guilt, 'you were only doing your job.' The Alsatian began to yowl. Then a light went on inside the house. *Time to leave.* Virgil high-tailed it down the gap between the garages and unbolted the gate. As he ran down the street, the photograph of June Dauber nearly slipped out of the pouch on his hoodie. He caught it and jammed it under his belt, ignoring its chafing. As he reached his bike, he realised that Windermere Way was a cul-de-sac. He was going to have to cycle past Dauber's house again to get out. *I did not think this through.*

There were lights on upstairs as the boy in black sped past number eighteen, but no one gave chase. When he hit country lanes, Virgil threw his head to the moon and howled louder than the Alsatian, basking in the glory of his success. The night air was still and cool. Imagining the look on Dauber's face when he awoke gave Virgil's goose bumps goose bumps, and playing the scenario out in his head sustained him all the way back to the bungalow. Tonight had been a warning shot. He had taught his enemy what it was to feel vulnerable.

All that remained to be seen was how Daniel Dauber would react.

~   ~   ~

In the morning, Virgil made a big show of finding the wallet and phone under the letterbox.

'Look! They must have had second thoughts during the night!'

Zelda was pacified but still ranted about the Daubers over breakfast. By the evening, she had calmed down significantly and even paused the telly so that they could pray for Daniel. *'He's a lost soul after all.'* Virgil marvelled again at his mother's capacity for forgiveness. Zelda's faith brought out the best in her.

Days passed, then a week. Dauber was a no-show. He was inactive on social media and Virgil hadn't seen him or his parasitic friends in Prestley at all. The weather continued to scorch, making most afternoons a sweltering blur of boxer shorts and iced drinks.

Since Ben Pidgeon's discharge from hospital, he and Virgil had been inseparable. Pidge came for tea on the Monday of the first week of the holidays. Zelda was on form and cooked a delicious lasagne. She positively beamed when Pidge smacked his lips and asked for more. She even let the boys finish off the lemon meringue back in Virgil's room—something that would *never* usually happen. Virgil knew his mum was thrilled for him. Pidge was the first real friend he'd had in years. He looked at the boy he had feared so much, slouching on his desk chair as they booted up the PlayStation. There was a mole on his fleshy neck with three hairs on it. From the stories Pidge told, Dauber and the gang were bigger monsters than Virgil had given them credit for. One anecdote about tying a firework to a cat had stuck with him. *It's no wonder he wanted out.*

'Pidge?'

'Yeah?'

'I'm thinking of taking up a martial art. For self-defence, but maybe even… to use in public.'

Pidge paused the game. 'What, like a crime-fighter?'

'Exactly. I'm so sick of sitting back, you know? I want to take action.'

Pidge fiddled with the controller, then said, 'Look up Krav Maga. Here,' he tossed his phone over. 'Unlimited data.'

Virgil cast a wary eyeball over his new friend to make sure he wasn't joking. Then opened the phone browser and keyed in the words. The description touted Krav Maga as a hybrid martial art. Difficult to learn, but once mastered, it was ruthless. It wasn't the most elegant of systems, lacking the flashiness of say, Kung Fu, but Virgil admired its brutal efficiency.

They spent the next few evenings watching training videos and practising on each other. The tutorials were made by an ex-military Israeli who had biceps three times the size of Virgil's thighs. He wasn't sure whether he was getting the moves right as most of them involved incapacitating a partner, and because of Pidge's pencil wound, they were limited in how physical they could get. To remedy this, they set about making a dummy. Using the stand and pole from a swing-ball, several coat hangers and some unused futons from the loft. They fashioned a makeshift human being. After duct-taping one of Tony's old jackets around the wobbly companion, Virgil was finally able to apply his developing portfolio against something the same height and shape—*and arguably the same intelligence*—as Daniel Dauber. They christened the dummy "Daniel Dorker" and went about setting up all kinds of unlikely scenarios in the garden, much to Zelda's amusement.

'What're you doing? Training for the Army?'

There were so many manoeuvres, holds, throws, kicks, punches and fall-breaks to learn, it made Virgil's head spin. The two he was having particular trouble with were the axe kick, and "escape from a mounted hold", but he was getting quicker with the hand to hand stuff, favouring the palm strike because it didn't hurt his knuckles so much. It went without saying that he left Goldie off during training.

Pidge even taught Virgil some of his own techniques. His personal favourite was one called THE WOBLE, which involved bracing your opponent's forearm, then pushing hard on the elbow until it popped the wrong way. He practised this one exclusively on Daniel Dorker as Pidge refused to lose an arm.

~ ~ ~

Virgil realised early on that the Ram mask would not be a viable real-world option. For a start, it was heavy and wouldn't stay on his face if he were running, *or fighting*. Also, it was an heirloom. Thanks to Goldie, Virgil's nose would not break upon contact with a baseball bat, but the old wooden mask would. His solution: 3D print an indestructible ram, but based on the prices of online freelancers, Virgil realised that he would need considerable cash-flow to fund this venture.

Sharing his thoughts with an excitable Pidge, they spent an evening brainstorming job ideas. Pidge suggested multiple ways of making a quick buck, none of which were legal. His brother, Trent, was a well-connected drug dealer and, according to Pidge, was bringing in around fifty thousand a year.

'You could be, like, an intern!'

'Or an in*mate*! I don't need *that* kind of money, Pidge. The 3D print is a few hundred quid. Anyway, drug dealers are exactly the kind of people I'm trying to bring down.'

'Oh, yeah…'

'Maybe I could turn a blind eye to Trent. Him being your brother and all.'

In the end, they settled on mowing lawns around Prestley. Virgil loved trundling out his dad's petrol mower at the bungalow. It was methodical, satisfying, and gave him time to think. *I've got the whole Summer too. If the demand is there, I could make a pretty penny.* Knowing his new friend was a dab hand at graphics, he asked Pidge to design him a flyer. Even on Zelda's rudimentary laptop, he was able to create a half-decent leaflet.

LAW-N-ORDER.

Need your grass cutting and your garden neatening up?

Call 01332 564778 for a free quote.

Friendly neighbourhood gardener.

Find me on Instagram and Facebook.

By the time the first week was up, they had printed several hundred flyers at the library, and guillotined them ready for distribution. As much as Virgil tried to convince him, Pidge was reluctant to join the outfit. He felt that his presence would discredit the whole endeavour.

'Most people are used to chasing me off their property, not inviting me onto it!'

Virgil arranged with Zelda that every morning he would get up early and begin mowing before the sun got fierce. On the first week of the holidays, Pidge gave him a hand flyering the village, and as the calls began to drip in, the diary filled up. By the second week, he was taking bookings two weeks in advance.

Virgil enjoyed the work. Most gardens were straightforward; a front and back lawn. He emptied the cuttings into people's green bins and did any edging work with a long pair of clippers he had borrowed off Mick. Virgil averaged about four houses a day, and on Pidge's advice, started to book people in based on their proximity to existing jobs. This meant wasting less time dragging the mower between properties, especially if one job was up by St Justus and the next down at Lowland Acre.

He charged £10 for an average-sized lawn and £15 for front and back. On a couple of the bigger houses, he tentatively suggested £30 for the lot. No one ever turned him down. The McAllisters had a good reputation in Prestley, and people were only too happy to support the boy they saw pushing his disabled mother to church every week.

Soon, Virgil was in a position to order the ram replica. He took detailed measurements of the original, photographing it from every angle. Then started to solicit quotes. It took a few false starts, but eventually, he found success with a Chinese PhD student in Edinburgh, who was doing a bit of freelance printing to supplement his income.

Liang Chung advised that for both flexibility and durability, nylon would be the choicest filament to use. He readily accepted the photographs and drawings, explaining that his research project was slow-moving and he loved a challenge. Best of all, Liang quoted Virgil only £100 to get the job done, assuring him of a full refund were the mask not fit for purpose. Virgil wrote back and said that he would send £200 upon completion, with the understanding that Liang kept their partnership hush-hush. *Pretty soon, people are going to recognise that mask.*

Liang agreed, but for an added layer of protection, Virgil conducted the entire correspondence under a fake name: Daniel Dorker. For delivery, he gave the address of an abandoned farmhouse on the outskirts of Prestley and stipulated that Liang informed him of the exact postage date. The PhD estimated a three-week wait. That placed the mask's arrival one week before the end of the holidays.

Time began to gallop. If Virgil wasn't mowing lawns or staking out Asda, he was with Pidge, who had started to invite him over. Pidge's house was situated on the north side of Prestley, not far from the rocky precipice of Widows Peak. The barbed cliff edge loomed over the Pidgeon household, casting a perpetual shadow over the row of red-bricked houses for much of the day. The boys spent most of their time in Pidge's bedroom playing videogames and avoiding Trent.

During the daytimes, Goldie stayed tucked away in Virgil's sock drawer. He couldn't risk being seen with her, after all, she was stolen goods. But curiosity clung to him. He found himself thinking about her all the time, wondering how she worked, what her limits were. *Unlimited power.* Most of all, he puzzled over the dragging footsteps. What else had been down there? Did it know what he had taken? Did it care?

CHAPTER TWENTY-ONE

FALLING FROM HEIGHTS

Virgil fastened Goldie tightly around his upper arm and slid the VIRGILANTE diary out from under the desk. Flicking to the section where he had drawn St Clavius, he scanned down the list of completed tests:

Razor blade, kitchen knife, saw, moving bandsaw, pizza slicer.

All the blades went blunt against my skin. The bandsaw snapped on my little finger.

Gas flame. Wood fire. Petrol fire. Hand in oven. Touch grill.

Hot to the touch, no damage to skin. Petrol on my arm burned itself out. N.B. Clothes ruined.

Boiling water. Pour on hand. Drink it.

No pain. Like sipping hot chocolate, without the chocolate.

Drop breeze block on bare toes.

Need to buy Dad new breeze blocks.

The most recent tests Virgil had done came under the heading: **Falling from heights.**

Over the last three days, he had jumped from a second-storey window. Thrown himself off spinney bridge, and leapt from the rooftop of the multi-storey car park in Oldley. Each time, he had picked himself up with zero breaks or bruises. In Oldley, he had cracked the pavement.

Giving a satisfied grunt at his progress, he scrolled a finger down the list of remaining trials:

Falling from heights: electricity pylon

Large electric shock.

Hit by moving vehicle. 30mph. 50mph. 70mph?

Drowning.

Hypothermia (test in Winter).

Gunshot.

These were all that he could think of. He was sure there were more ways to die, but the list covered most bases. Lack of courage had proven the biggest hurdle—it had taken him thirty minutes to jump off the multi-storey car park. But after a successful first attempt, he did it again for the sheer thrill of it. There was something terrible about actively trying to injure oneself; Virgil had such a natural aversion to it that he had to train himself to shut down any survival instincts. Goldie had kept him safe so far.

His Casio beeped one AM. With a well-practised manoeuvre, he tucked the diary out of sight and slipped on his jacket, zipping his mobile in the breast pocket just in case. Then he opened the window wide. He had placed an old stone bench just outside; it was the side of the house that his mum never used. This meant no more sneaking out through the front door, which was much riskier.

Five minutes later, he was zipping merrily down Monk's Lane. The country road wound its way South of Prestley and past the forest of lowland acre. It wasn't the forest he needed tonight; Virgil was aiming for the huge electricity pylons dotted along the valley. The first accessible one was a kilometre south of the village. After cycling for ten minutes, he caught his first glimpse of the tower. It squatted imposingly in the centre of a dark field, an uncompromising lattice of welded steel.

By the time Virgil had stowed his bike in a ditch and reached the base, he was exhausted. The ground was muculent clay and, despite weeks of sunshine, boggy patches still existed at random. His trainers were caked in sticky clumps and weighed triple what they should. With breathless relief, he laid hand to a metal leg of the pylon and craned his neck. Thick black lines crisscrossed with mathematical precision against a backlit spray of milky way. A faint buzzing seemed to radiate from the very ground at his feet. He squelched over to the ladder, jumping and pulling himself onto the bottom few rungs which were raised five feet or so above ground level. Once he was up, he used the sharp edge of the ladder to scrape off some mud. Then he began to climb.

The ascent was long and monotonous and the rungs bit into Virgil's palms—icy and unforgiving on his bare skin. The higher he got, the more agonising it became, until he was stopping every twenty pulls to breathe on them. *Maybe cold is Goldie's weakness. Better leave that hypothermia test until last.* With the field so dark, it was difficult to tell how high he was. But the breeze intensified and a few startled birds almost made him lose his footing. *At least I won't be climbing down.*

When the ladder ended, it was all narrow struts and gaping chasms. Acres of sticky mud surrounded the lonely lookout like a sea of marmite. He clambered gracelessly to the outside of the pylon, looking for a good place to leap from. It seemed impossible to find a spot where the curvature of the metal didn't place the pylon's deep-rooted legs in the way of his trajectory. Virgil's eye was drawn to the hazy lights of Prestley. The hill village dominated the horizon, with St Justus' spires puncturing the night sky like some gothic version of the Disney logo.

Blowing out in long, hard gusts, Virgil began to psyche himself up. He slipped a frozen finger under his shirt to make sure his insurance policy was still tightly fastened. The high wind wailed all around him, building to a crescendo, egging him on. He began the countdown.

It was over. The air rushed around his joggers as he plummeted feet-first through the darkness. Then the ground swallowed him up with a hefty slurp and Virgil was up to his armpits in bog. He tried to move his legs but couldn't. In fact, he couldn't move his body at all. The soft clay had accepted his hundred-metre pencil-jump as readily as cork accepts a dart. His legs were driven in deep. With every attempt he made to wrench himself free, he could feel a field's worth of suction pulling against him. *You have got to be kidding me!*

He struggled for an unspecified amount of time, getting muddier and muddier until both his arms and face were plastered in the freezing sludge. Close to despairing, Virgil managed to squeeze his hand into his jacket's breast pocket and extract his phone. His fingers were too caked to properly input on the touch screen, but with a few deft presses of his nose, he was able to bring up the one contact who might be able to help.

Pidge always kept his phone on. Even at night. Virgil pressed *Call* with his nose and willed his best friend to pick up. The dialling tone, five rings, then…

'Hello?'

'Pidge. Mate. I'm in a bit of a pickle. Well, actually, I'm completely stuck and, I'm sorry, I know it's late, and I wouldn't normally ask, but... I really need your help.' He finished despondently.

Pidge yawned. Virgil could almost see him stretching as he shrugged on a jumper.

'Where are you, buddy? I'll be there as quick as I can.'

CHAPTER TWENTY-TWO

SECRETS

It was 4 AM and the two boys were sitting at Pidge's kitchen table; a disc of polished oak with a forlorn-looking fruit bowl in the centre. Virgil didn't speak for a long while. He was still shivering, wrapped in a towel his friend had grabbed from the airing cupboard. Both he and Pidge were brown from top to toe. They had thrashed around together in the mud, Pidge heaving on the climbing rope he had brought, while Virgil tried desperately to wriggle free of the bog's glutinous clutches. After much grunting and straining, he had surfaced with a huge pop. Too frozen to speak, the boys had clumped back to the hedgerow and ridden back to Pidge's house in silence.

It wasn't until he got off his mountain bike that Virgil realised his shoe was missing. *Twenty quid, lost in the middle of some stupid field. You idiot.*

'Gonna tell me what you were doing out there, playing stuck in the mud?' Pidge's mouth was joking, but the kink in his eyebrows wasn't.

Virgil wrapped the warm towel a little tighter, then said,

'First, so grateful that you came. I c-c-c-c-can't tell you how awful it was being stranded out there in the dark.'

Pidge shook his head in a 'not-at-all' kind of way.

'No, really, Ben,' insisted Virgil, 'I was starting to go c-c-crazy out there, imagining stuff—things creeping across the field towards me. When I heard your bike and saw the torch, I knew I was safe. It was the biggest relief. Honestly, mate.'

'What're friends for? You big brown freak!' Pidge said, then stopped himself, horrified, 'I meant the mud. Oh, sorry, I was meaning the—you're covered in brown mud. I'm so sorry.'

Virgil batted it away. 'Don't be stupid! I know you meant the mud! And even if you didn't, I am brown, and a freak!'

Pidge relaxed again, slouching bashfully in his chair.

'Anyway, the reason you were stuck in a field at 3 AM?'

'You have to trust me,' Virgil urged. 'Because this is going to sound insane.'

Pidge crossed his filthy legs and made a triangle with his fingers, leaning forward. 'Trust you? I trust you. Why? What have you found out there? Buried treasure?'

'Not quite. It was the pylon I was interested in. You see, the reason you found me sunk up to my frozen nips… was because… I climbed the pylon to the top… and jumped off.'

Pidge blinked furiously as if he had misheard. Then his face transformed into the epitome of pity.

'Oh, mate. I'm so sorry, I mean I've been there too. When Mum and Dad split and we left our old house, it was the lowest I've ever been.'

'Ben, Pidge, Pidge, Pidge. No. I'm not suicidal. I was testing something.'

Pidge looked thunderstruck. Slowly, Virgil lifted up his encrusted sleeve to reveal Goldie shimmering beneath.

'Holy Codfish,' muttered Pidge, 'Mithril!'

'I know, right?' Virgil slid it off and passed it across the table. It felt strange letting someone else hold her, touch her. She had protected him from so much already. But Pidge could be trusted. *It's only right that I share my secret.*

'Put it on,' Virgil encouraged him.

'What just on my arm like this?'

'Yup, now pass me your lighter.'

'Virgil, you know I quit. I vape now, I—oh alright, here you go.' He slid the worn green lighter over to Virgil, who sparked it to life. The flame flickered in the dim kitchen, throwing all kinds of unsteady shapes onto the tiles.

'Hold your hand out.' Virgil demonstrated with his own. Pidge copied. 'Now,' said Virgil, 'this is the trust bit. Whatever I do next. Don't move that hand.'

He brought the undulating flame steadily towards Pidge's downturned palm. As he did so, the boys locked eyes across the table, miniscule reflections of the fire dancing in their wide pupils. As the flame went under his hand, Pidge bit his lip but managed to hold steady. After a second or two, his trembling hand regained its composure. With a look of utter bewilderment, he turned it over and over in the yellow blaze. The flame licked at his fingers, coursing up the back of his hand as if it were a fresh piece of kindling, but never charring, never blackening.

'It's warm,' breathed Pidge, 'but I'm not in agony… how? How can it not be hurting?' With a profound moment of realisation, his mouth hung open and he touched the golden shield strap on his arm. 'It's magic, it's a magic armband!'

'Keep your voice down!' Virgil cast his eyes warily to the ceiling.

'Oh, don't worry,' Pidge was buzzing, 'Dad and Chrissy are in Edinburgh and Trent's working in the city. It's just us.' He lifted Goldie up, tracing the beautiful markings. 'What else can it do? Wait. No, no, no, noooo. You said you were jumping off the pylon!' Pidge pointed an incredulous finger. 'Are you telling me that this… *thing*, protected you?'

Virgil was grinning like a man who had won the lottery. He nodded.

'What! What?! This is just… this is just…'

'Amazing? Incredible? Like something out of a comic book?'

'Well, yeah!' finished Pidge, utterly puffed out. He handed Goldie back. 'Show me what else it can do.'

The two boys spent a happy half hour taking it in turns wearing Goldie then straight up trying to murder each other. Steak knives bounced off their chests with ease, a drill on hammer mode couldn't penetrate Pidge's bicep, and the iron—whacked up to its hottest setting—didn't even hiss when Virgil pressed it against his own ear. The finale was Pidge returning from upstairs with Trent's air rifle. Virgil went and stood at the far end of the lounge, while Pidge loaded up and took aim. After the shot, they found the bullet under the sofa, flattened. Pidge emptied the gun into Virgil several other times before swapping places. Then Virgil perched carefully on an armchair and told Pidge the whole story—Dauber, the crypt, everything. He left nothing out, not even the shuffling steps.

'Creepy,' Pidge whispered.

Virgil's watch beeped five AM.

'Crud, Mum gets up for work in an hour. How am I going to explain these clothes?'

'No worries. Our bathroom's upstairs, first door you come to. You strip off and chuck your clothes down. I'll get them washed and you can borrow some of my stuff to ride home in.'

They fist-bumped. Virgil gushing, 'You're the best.'

He was showered and dressed in no time. Pidge's clothes were baggy; he had to put the belt on its tightest setting just to keep his jeans up. But it felt so awesome to be provided for in this way that Virgil didn't care one bit. He bade Pidge farewell, thanking him again profusely, then cycled home.

He reached the bungalow just as the first canary rays were catching St Justus' spire, and was up and through the window by five-forty-five. He slid out the diary and grabbed a fine liner.

Falling from heights: electricity pylon.

Check.

CHAPTER TWENTY-THREE

THE PASTOR'S WIFE

With all the time he was spending on Goldie, Virgil was careful not to neglect his pursuit of the Saxo lads. Making himself a fake Facebook profile, he uploaded a picture of a random skinhead. He called his creation Craig Kirk. Then he friend-requested a ton of local ne'er-do wells and joined a bunch of morally questionable groups, including Keep Britain British and the ARI. If he was going to track down Skull Sleeves and his crew, he would have to move in the same hellish circles, online at least. As the friend acceptances began to accrue, he sifted through thousands of images, looking for a face he recognised.

Then, almost entirely by accident, he came across a goldmine: an anonymously-run group called Spotted Oldley. The bulk of the posts were lost cats or long rants about noisy youths and barbeque smoke. But by carefully studying the historical irks of Oldley's residents, Virgil was able to build a picture of his home town. Going back through five years' worth of posts, he began to make notes, screenshotting key images and jotting down all kinds of character descriptions and eye-witness accounts. Before long, the VIRGILANTE diary was nearing capacity. Certain characters stood out and even had multiple posts devoted to their anti-social behaviour. A man in a grey boiler suit had been seen fly-tipping more than once. Then there were varied descriptions of a youth on a distinctive green motorbike who had been shoplifting and driving erratically around the industrial estate. There were shaky videos of street fights filmed from second-storey windows and even CCTV of an attempted robbery. Virgil didn't include the missing pets, but anything that seemed suspicious or even slightly dodgy, he noted down.

One thing kept cropping up: the vaguely terrifying tales of an old woman who seemed to exist at the fringes of the communities' posting habits. Never the focus of a story, this small 'watcher woman' or 'kindly grandmother' was often mentioned in relation to unsuccessful crimes. There she would be, helping at the scene of a road traffic collision or sitting with someone while they awaited the emergency services. She seemed to disappear whenever the author of the post wanted to thank her, so many had taken to the group in order to voice their appreciation. The entire idea of a ghostly grannie made Virgil smirk. But even so, he put the hockey stick in front of his door that night, just in case.

~ ~ ~

Reports of impending mega-storms flooded the newspapers and radio stations. But despite the Met-office issuing an amber weather warning, the sun continued to bake Prestley. The extended dry spell was making lawn-mowing easy. Virgil found himself whizzing over large patches of grass in as little as twenty minutes, and with the clippings moisture-less and light, the mower needed minimal scraping. He made short work of his bookings.

Now that Goldie's big secret was out, he and Pidge spent more time outside, dreaming up fresh experiments together. Two weeks passed. Virgil was counting down the days until the mask arrived. There had been radio silence from Liang Chung, but he took this as encouragement. *No news is good news.*

One obstacle that they faced was criminal surveillance. Batman had a signal, Peter Parker had his spider-sense, police got 999 calls. But as Virgil trod his patch, keeping his eyes peeled, he began to realise just how grounded he was. With only his feet and his rusty red mountain bike, it was much harder to patrol an area in the same way that his fictional heroes could.

One afternoon, while they were tying firecrackers to each other, he expressed these concerns. Pidge rubbed his chubby hands together: 'I have got something to show you. If I'm going to be your sidekick—'

Virgil snorted, 'Sorry?'

'Every hero has a sidekick, Virgil. If I'm going to help, then we'll need some proper tech. Follow me.'

They went inside, the red firecrackers clattering off their ankles like explosive wind chimes. Up in Pidge's bedroom, he stretched, reaching down a box from the top of his wardrobe, 'I took the liberty of buying us an assistant. Out of the brown parcel and polystyrene pads, he unboxed a dark grey drone. He had even taken the time to Tippex a Ram onto its base.

'Whaaat? How much was that?'

'Few hundred. I er, *borrowed* a couple of rolls from Trent's room and he never even noticed. I had left-over vouchers from Christmas too,' he added as if this mitigated the spending of drug money.

'This. Is. Awesome.' Virgil lifted the drone tentatively. Pidge buzzed a couple of rotors to make him jump.

'Flippity jip, Pidge! I almost dropped the ruddy thing!'

'She's more robust than she looks. Look, there's an inbuilt HD camera.' Pidge held the drone out of his bedroom window, then sent it straight up into the sky. He turned the remote towards Virgil. On the screen between his thumb-sticks there showed an aerial view of the village.

'I was saving it for our first patrol together. As a surprise. Might be helpful to have an eye in the sky.'

'Incredible. So, I'm pounding the streets, and you're in some control centre somewhere…'

'I could stay right here, she's got a five-mile radius so that covers Prestley easily. We'd have to think more carefully about Oldley.'

'Right, but how do we stay in contact without racking up a crazy phone bill?'

'Yeah,' Pidge kicked his feet, 'I've thought of that too.'

Virgil cocked an eyebrow. 'You're really getting into this, aren't you?'

'Can you blame me? You found a magic armband!'

'It's not magic, or an armband. Well, maybe it is magic, but I've been thinking about strapping it around my leg instead. What's the comms solution then?'

'Walkie-talkie earbuds. You can get them on eBay now for around fifty quid. Hunters use them out in Canada for conversations across a forest without spooking the deer. I saw it on a documentary.'

Six months ago, the idea of Pidge watching a documentary would have sparked laughter in Virgil. As it was, he was discovering hidden depths to the guy on an almost daily basis. He swallowed a joke about Bambi not being a documentary, and instead opted for, 'Awesome. You've thought it all through!'

A smile crept to the corners of Pidge's mouth and he shrugged modestly. Virgil suspected that he wasn't used to being complimented and made a mental note to do it more often. Pidge made one big ugly flower, but boy was he blossoming.

~ ~ ~

It was the penultimate Saturday of the Summer holidays and Virgil was mowing a lawn on Chancel Street. When he stopped to gulp away at the ice-cold peach juice

Mrs Crabble had brought out, he noticed that the house across the road was derelict. The paint on the weathered fascia was flaking and the grass on its front looked more jungle than lawn. It was spilling out onto the pavement. All the curtains were drawn and a beige rover with rust damage was squeezed into the tiny carport.

Spotting a business opportunity. Virgil quickly finished Mrs Crabble's gardens, then enquired about the owner of the ramshackle semi.

'Oh, that's Floyd Burlock's house,' she said, disapprovingly.

Virgil was stunned, and his face must have shown it. For Mrs Crabble quickly readjusted her expression and said, 'Do you know Floyd?'

'No, no,' he coughed, 'not to speak to anyway.' He wiped a hand on the back of his jeans. 'Do you think he would like his lawn mowing?'

'I should think he would! Very much so!' Mrs Crabble nodded vigorously. 'It's not like Floyd to let the grass get out of hand, especially given his job.'

'Why, what does he do?'

'Well, he's retired now. Like most of us on the street. But he used to be a gardener. Ran his own landscaping firm up near the Spindles. Latterly, he was the gardener up at the church.'

'At St Justus?'

'Yes.'

'Do you know why he stopped working there?'

Mrs Crabble eyed Virgil keenly for a moment.

'I don't like to be one to gossip, young man,' she straightened the sleeve of her cardigan (how she was wearing one in this heat was anyone's guess), then she began. 'I've never been a churchgoer myself. But the rumour at the Women's Institute was that Floyd had a fling with the Pastor's wife.' She sucked her lips in as if she had said too much, but Virgil could tell she was enjoying it. She watched his reaction closely.

'Pastor Jerome's wife? Mrs Yeboah?'

'Margaery. A gentle soul, she chaired our WI meetings. She was very interested in the past, she knew all about the history of the village. It was a real loss when she left. Must be coming up for twelve years now.'

'Sorry, Mrs Crabble, I'm a little confused. I had always been under the impression that Mrs Yeboah died.'

'Yes, well, bit of a scandal when it all kicked off. I can imagine the congregation wanting to keep it hush-hush.

Might've been easier for the Pastor if she *had* kicked the proverbial! Oh!' she shook her head, 'I must apologise, that is a terrible thing to say.'

'So, where is she if she's still alive?'

'Felicity Gardens I heard.'

'What's Felicity Gardens?'

'A psychiatric hospital down South, Cornwall I think.' She folded her arms to signal the conversation was over. Virgil was still reeling and sat down on Mrs Crabble's garden wall. The old lady picked up the tray and empty glass. 'It was a big shock to all of us when it came out— the affair—the pressure must have got to Margaery because it drove her quite mad. It was only a month or two later that she was shipped off to the loony bin. Oops, you're not meant to call them that anymore, are you? Anyway,' she looked with disdain at the house opposite, 'Floyd Burlock has been shunned by the village ever since.'

Virgil took his money in silence, bowing his head in thanks before trundling home in a daze. He felt as if the earth had tilted and everything was off-kilter. *Margaery Yeboah, the Pastor's wife.* Suddenly, he understood why Jerome didn't believe in karma.

CHAPTER TWENTY-FOUR

CATFISHING

It was hard to know how to bring up Mrs Yeboah with his mum. At tea, Virgil was working on a conversation starter that could Segway easily into the subject. When the words wouldn't come, he contented himself with cutting up Maisie's grapes and making them into a smiley face on her plate. She giggled and said, 'Man.' Then scoffed them all in her inimitable way.

He was just getting up the courage to ask when his phone vibrated in his pocket. Zelda didn't allow mobiles at the dinner table, but while she was over at the hob, Virgil sneaked a look, assuming it to be Pidge—the only person who texted him apart from O2. It was Facebook; a friend request for Craig Kirk. He tapped the little blue icon and the app loaded up. The image that accompanied the notification made his heart enter a skipping competition.

Scowling at the camera in the reflection of a wardrobe mirror was a lad with his shirt off. A side light threw shade on his skinny chest, exaggerating the sparsely populated muscles. His top lip had the shadings of an eleven-year-old, but he was as pasty as they came. A thick gold chain hung around his neck and his backwards cap was plastered with gang symbols. It was the teeth though—in all their unbrushed yellow glory—that jogged Virgil's memory. This was one of the Saxo lads, one-hundred percent. He knew it from the boiling sensation in the pit of his stomach. This was the scum who had bent double with laughter as his mum was wheeled to and fro.

Damian Wurzel sent you a friend request. Accept. Decline.

Virgil pressed accept without hesitation. He could scarcely believe it. Fishing at the shallow end of the gene pool, and at long last, a bite! *Well, well, well, Damian, nice to meet you.*

'Virgil! No phones at the table,' Zelda pinned him with a cross look.

'Sorry,' he muttered, stowing it.

The rest of the meal dragged into eternity. The only thing on Virgil's mind was getting back upstairs to sift through Damian Wurzel's associates. He couldn't focus on anything that his mum was saying, and got by on grunts and yeahs, appropriately spaced and at key intervals.

Later, as he was washing the dishes, Zelda rolled over and put a hand on his back.

'Are you alright, darling? You don't seem yourself.'

He couldn't tell her about his breakthrough. Instead, he settled for something that would stop the conversation dead in its tracks.

'I just miss Dad.'

Zelda's hand froze and shrunk away. There was an intake of breath, and then she said,

'I know, love.' Then more quietly, 'I know.' She started to wipe the table down, 'If I'm honest, I miss him too. It's not right that we are apart. But,' she swallowed, 'your father has had it rough with everything that's happened, he needs time to sort himself out. I'm sure he'll come back. Jerome thinks so too.'

Virgil lifted a dripping plate onto the rack and faced her, wiping his hands on his apron. He was shocked to hear her speak so kindly about his dad. Usually, the mere mention of him would extinguish the conversation like a fag dropped in a puddle. Hope stirred within—his parents might still have a chance together. Nothing would make him happier.

The mention of Jerome spurred Virgil to ask his burning question.

'I was speaking to a lady this morning over on Chancel Street; Mrs Crabby, or Crapple or something. Crabble! That's it! Anyway, we got onto talking about St Justus… She told me that Margaery Yeboah had been sent away to a psych hospital. Is that true? The way everyone speaks at Church, I had honestly thought she was dead.'

Naked shock registered on Zelda's round face. She clearly had not expected *that*. She looked down, weighing her options.

'We tried to shield you from it,' she said hesitantly. 'Growing up at St Justus… it was an ugly, ugly scandal. Dad and I, we just didn't think you needed to know. I'm sorry you found out from some village gossip rather than from us.'

'Mrs Crabble said that Margaery had an affair with Floyd Burlock.'

Zelda's lips made a thin line as she smacked them, 'Yup. Your father was ecstatic when you found the hat with blood on it.'

'He was?' asked Virgil, incredulous.

'Dad was Church Warden when it all came out, he resigned over the leadership's handling of the issue. He always felt that Burlock got away scot-free whilst Margaery...'

'Lost her marbles?'

'Mmm,' said Zelda, then, 'I still can't believe it was true. It just wasn't *her*. Margaery always said the same as all the rest of us: Floyd gave her the creeps.'

'If she's alive, why does no one talk about her? We don't even pray for her from the front.'

'It does seem strange, yes, but then, you have to consider the pain it causes Jerome. Plus, the majority of the congregation grew up in a time where the best way to squash a scandal was to never discuss it. As far as most people are concerned, Margaery Yeboah is taboo; a dark corner of the Church's past.'

'Hmm.' Virgil pondered to himself. *It doesn't add up, Jerome banishing his wife, mental health issues or not. It doesn't ring true.* When the washing up was done, he threw himself onto his bed, phone out and thumbs working rapidly. He scrolled through Damian Wurzel's five-hundred and four friends.

Within the hour, he had all four Saxo lads' names. He wrote them on a fresh page and sellotaped it on the inside cover of the VIRGILANTE diary

Targets.

Damian Wurzel – *yellow-toothed, snot-nosed, weasel-looking skinhead with a diamond ear stud.*

Kade Wurzel – *Damian's older brother: same haircut, squarer head. No piercings. He pushed Mum in the car park.*

Benjamin Gill – *the Michael Peña-looking one, I bit him.*

Patrick Jones – *AKA Skull Sleeves: the Saxo driver. He filmed it all.*

As the three remaining Saxo lads each accepted his friend requests, Virgil noted down every scrap of information from their pages, including places of employment and the venues they frequented. Before long, he had built up a profile for each one. Now, all he needed was an excuse to meet in person.

He decided to make real-life contact with Damian first—after all, it was old yellow-tooth who had fallen into his lap at the dinner table. *I can scare Damian, use him to let the others know they are being hunted. Let it be a prophecy of doom. Let them sweat for a while before judgment.*

Over a series of awkward emails, he arranged to meet Damian at the ARI march in Oldley Town centre on Saturday. The conversation went along the lines of, *'Hi, I'm Craig, good to meet another true Englishman. Fancy a drink before we go burka-bashing?'* ARI stood for Against Radical Islam, and was an organisation comprised of ex and current football hooligans. They raged against the Muslims 'coming over here and ruining our culture' and would demonstrate by holding peaceful marches where they smashed up their favourite pubs and anyone else who got in the way. Realistically, ARI events were just an excuse for violence. Recently, their focus had shifted to the country's borders and most people agreed that, nowadays, ARI might just as well stand for Against Rescuing Immigrants. As far as Zelda was concerned, ARI stood for All Really Ignorant, and Virgil was forbidden from going anywhere near Oldley while the march was in progress.

Damian was well up for a bit of racially-motivated violence, and eagerly accepted. They would meet in the Joiner's Arms at two. The march began there. *Whew, is he going to get a shock when a Jamaican kid pulls up a bar stool.* Technically, Virgil was too young to be necking pints with Damian and his Neo-Nazi buddies. But Goldie had given him a new sense of freedom. *If the barman won't serve me, he'll have a hard time getting me to leave.*

Virgil didn't go out that night. He was too exhausted from the day's revelations. In the early hours, his phone pinged. Through blurry eyes, he saw that Liang Chung had emailed. The Ram mask was finished and would arrive later that day at the abandoned farmhouse. Chung had also attached a photograph, but Virgil didn't open it. He wanted the first time he saw the mask to be its unwrapping. *Perfect timing, Liang Chung, I hope you smash that PhD.*

It would not be long before he could crack criminal skulls with total anonymity.

CHAPTER TWENTY-FIVE

THE JOINER'S ARMS

The Joiner's Arms was heaving. The entire taxi rank outside the pub was blocked by a police van and two horses. A fog of smoke lingered, perpetuated by the countless bald apes in football shirts who stood around, glaring at anything that moved.

Virgil leaned back into the cover of his vantage point. With a movement that was becoming instinctual, he felt around his thigh for Goldie. She sat comfortingly above the knee, his insurance policy against getting ground into the pavement. He checked his rucksack. Ram mask MK II stared back. Even in the shade of this alleyway, the glow-in-the-dark frosting was doing its job. Liang had delivered and then some—that man deserved his PhD. In order to bolster the mask's security, Virgil had hand-sewn it to a balaclava. This gave the sides and back of his head coverage and was more comfortable than the nylon strap.

'I'm about to go to an ARI rally,' he said out loud in disbelief, 'I'm about to go to an ARI rally wearing a sheep mask.'

He scanned the front of the pub again. Cameras. There were cameras at each end of the building. He had not planned for that. But what to do? *This needs to be anonymous.* There was no telling how the situation might escalate inside, but judging by the clientele out here... Virgil took a calming breath and looked down at his clothes. He was dressed in denim shorts and a faded Derby County shirt. He hoped that they were generic enough to provide some semblance of camouflage. There would be no camouflaging his smooth hickory skin. He looked to the skies, *no sign of the drone yet.* Pidge was nearby, where exactly, Virgil didn't know. The earpieces hadn't arrived so they had no way of keeping in touch.

The Clocktower chimed two o'clock. *Party time.* He pulled on the Ram and walked around the block. Two police cars crawled past but took no notice of him. Coming up from the van rentals place which backed onto the beer garden, he pulled himself up onto the wall. The broken glass bottles which were set into the top did nothing to his palms, though they did snag his shirt. He dropped lightly onto the other side.

The beer garden was heaving. But by a stroke of luck, Virgil had landed behind a large planter overflowing with purple flowers. No one had noticed him yet. *OK. Got to be CCTV savvy, alter my walk slightly.* Trying to look confident, he swaggered toward the back doors. Many a mouth sagged open in slack-jawed astonishment as he passed. There was a brief vacuum of stunned silence, then the beer garden broke out into an angry buzz. As he reached the open fire exit, a bottle smashed on the door frame above his head, showering him with glass and a spray of Heineken. He cringed a little, then straightened his shoulders again, hoping they hadn't noticed. *Pull yourself together! No one in here can touch you.*

The place was rowdy, chock-full of England flags and sunburn. Virgil hung left and found himself in the main room and at the end of the long, polished bar. Every seat was filled. He could practically hear the bar stools groaning under the weight of so many red-blooded xenophobes. A drunken chorus of Rule-Britannia was in full swing as he darkened the doorway.

Before locating Damian Wurzel, he did a visual sweep of the ceiling. There was one camera pointed at the bar, the other had been turned to face the corner. Damian was sat at a table full of tracksuits with similar haircuts and builds to his own. Given the average BMI of the place, they looked like children.

Virgil took a moment on the threshold before anyone had seen him. He let his eyes burn into the side of Damian's head. *You laughed while they terrorised my mum. You laughed your yellow teeth off.* He checked that the Ram was covering his head and wove his way over.

There were no chairs free at Damian's table. *Better start strong.* Virgil tapped the spotty twenty-something closest to him, jabbed his thumb over his shoulder and said, in a voice much deeper than his own, 'MOVE.'

As the young man looked up—uncertainty slathered over his weasel features—Virgil realised that Rule-Britannia had come to an abrupt end. Every beady eye in the room was on him, every tendon in every engorged neck strained in his direction.

'The hell are you supposed to be?'

'You're in my seat. Last chance.'

Whatever the lad said next was rendered incomprehensible by the cacophonous laughter that shook the walls. As Virgil circled, he saw them all, banging their fists on the tables. They slapped each other on the back, doubled over, wheezed into their drinks.

'Boy's got a death wish.'

'You run out of chairs back in Africa?'

'Taking our jobs and our seats!'

'AHA AHA AHAAA HAHAHAHAAAAAAAA!' The noise was an assault on the ears—a gaudy, hellish sound. The lad's hand was around a fresh pint of Carling. Virgil put his hand on the top of the glass and applied a medium amount of pressure. The beasts roared their approval, great booming guffaws as grown men wept into the crooks of their arms.

Pint guy looked furiously at Virgil and mouthed some obscenities as he tried to pull his drink away. But the glass wouldn't budge. He tried again and again, his whole body shaking as he heaved at the beverage. Then he stood straight up and went for the punch. Too slow. Virgil's training kicked in and he leant away, catching the fist in his open palm. They dosie-do'd, swapping places. The lad went to pull his fist out but found that he couldn't. Keeping eye contact through the slits, Virgil began to squeeze.

Pint guy's knuckles popped like corn and both fingers and thumb crunched inward with a subdued clicking. His face became a well of horror. When he thought he had made his point, Virgil stopped squeezing. Without letting go, he leant over and picked up the beer.

The room had gone silent again. The only sound was an old guy dropping his cutlery as he stood up to watch. Virgil nudged the mask up to free his mouth and began to drink. Pins dropped. The beer tasted awful. He was not allowed alcohol at home and had never been invited to parties where it flowed. But the illusion had to be maintained. He wanted them to remember a man. Not a fifteen-year-old.

Pint guy's eyes were watering and he bared his teeth, hyperventilating through his nostrils. As Virgil finished the pint, he saw a miniscule version of his victim through the bottom of the glass. Something like pity stirred in him until he reminded himself that normally *he'd* have been the one in casualty. He finished and slammed the glass down.

Before releasing the pulverised hand, he said, 'What's your name?'

'Gggggeorge Davies.'

'George, I'd like another pint. Bring it back with spit in and I'll break your other hand.' He let go. The stunned silence continued. George made his way to the bar cradling his wrist and making soft moaning sounds.

Trembling uncontrollably with adrenaline, Virgil sat down. A sleek grey whippet trotted over and licked at his knee where some of the beer had dripped. Its owner called it sharply back. People were starting to talk again, bloodshot eyes bulged, looking him up and down. *This has to be done quickly.* He drummed his fingers on the table, then cocked his head towards—

'Damian!'

CHAPTER TWENTY-SIX

TO IMMIGRATION!

'Damian!' Virgil said genially, as if greeting an old friend, 'You probably don't recognise me with my mask on,' he offered his hand, 'Craig Kirk.'

'But… you're not… Craig Kirk is white.'

'Don't believe everything you see online, Damian.'

'What do you want me for? Who are you?'

'Oh, I'm very ordinary really. I care for my disabled mother, pick up her prescriptions, take her to the shops…'

Recognition dawned on Damian's face like a stop-motion sunrise.

'You're from the car park. From Asda car park.'

'Wow, that *has* saved us a lot of time!' Virgil retracted the hand, unshaken. 'Yes, Damian, I am. I must say, I'm disappointed you didn't save me a seat.' Damian sat dumbly, looking from Virgil to his own ashen-faced mates, to the sea of angry faces surrounding them. 'Aren't you going to say something, Damian? Don't you have *anything* you want to say to me?'

Damian found his tongue, 'This lot'll string you up. I seen them do it before.'

This was the moment, the perfect time to strike. Virgil knew he could shatter most of Damian's major limbs before the crowd stopped him. But there was something... something in the little rat's voice. He was shaking; visible tremors rattled off his body as he sat shrinking. '*I seen them do it before.*' This statement was not a threat, it was a warning. He was terrified for Virgil.

Suddenly, he saw Damian for what he really was: a stupid kid who had made stupid friends and stupid choices. Of course, he'd be at the ARI march, of course, he'd laugh while Mum was wheeled around. *He's just an idiot, a harmless idiot. Always in the idiot place at the idiot time doing the idiot thing.* Virgil decided Damian had received the message. He wouldn't hurt the guy. Suddenly, the plan to intimidate him in broad daylight with over one-hundred witnesses seemed very foolish.

The crowd were getting restless. Racist slurs were called from the back of the room. Virgil had never felt so self-conscious. Even masked, the pressure of being the focal point for so much hatred was making him burn up. Both front and back exits were crammed with bodies. Row upon row of thickset men, competing for a look at the soon-to-be-dead Jamaican. There were women too. Virgil made a decision: *I won't hurt the women.*

'Just for the record, Damian,' Virgil said quietly, 'I gave you the chance to apologise.'

George arrived with the beer. Virgil thanked him, grabbing the ice-cold pint and stepping from his chair onto the table. There was an uproar of wood on wood as the whole pub got to their feet. *Nobody* stood on tables in the Joiner's Arms, not without an England flag.

'WAIT!' Virgil shouted, making everyone jump. He pulled his mask back down and raised the glass, saluting their awestruck faces, 'To immigration!' he said. 'Cheers!'

Damian and his friends scrambled to get out of the way. Then the table was knocked out from under Virgil's feet and he was on his back. The wooden beams of the ceiling were replaced by grimacing faces. Instinctively, he shielded his head. All over him, he felt gentle impacts, like it was raining tennis balls. He opened his eyes to see fists and feet crashing down from every angle. Most of those who were stamping fell away quickly with cries of surprise. Toes crunched into the softness of his sides, and as he got to his feet, several elbows and kneecaps shattered against his forehead. He saw every blow coming and forced himself not to duck. The mob eventually took a break, many of them limping back to their seats, staring, confusedly at their grievous injuries.

Virgil stood in the centre of the room, surrounded by them.

The harsh tinkle of breaking glass. A woman staggered into the circle. She had a St George's flag painted onto her face and was wearing a leopard-skin tank top. She held the broken bottle behind her as if to conceal it.

'No,' Virgil tried to warn her, 'No don't because you'll—'

She lunged at his throat. The jagged ends splintered upon contact with his Adam's apple, driving themselves back into her hand. The woman gasped. Staring at the lacerations. Then she fainted, hitting her head on a table edge.

'Immigrant scum!' someone shouted.

Virgil knew that he could do some serious damage if he chose to. Goldie turned his wiry body into granite. He tried to ignore them, tried to brush aside their ignorance.

'Your mother was a filthy monkey!'

Virgil swung at the man who had said it. His fist connected with a loud crack, snapping the racist's glasses in half and his nose too. He fell back into the arms of his comrades, out for the count. Then Virgil took them on, all of them. They didn't come at him in ones and twos, they were ever-present, all-surrounding—a never-ending barrage of bellies and boot-ends. He lashed out indiscriminately, punching lungs and teeth and other fists. Everything that came into contact with his hands crumpled upon impact. Groans from the injured mingled with cries of surprise as strong men got beaten at their own game. When Virgil knew that he had put at least thirty people in casualty, he slowed down. The very last thing he wanted to do was kill someone. That was a line he could not cross.

Then he saw something that made his stomach drop. Standing on a table at the back of the room was a man with his phone out. He had been filming the entire thing. *I've got to get that phone.*

Without warning, another twenty men piled in through the front doors. Before he could turn around, they were onto him, crushing down in a pile-on of beer stains and sweat patches. He bent his knees and pushed up, lifting six men off his shoulders and throwing one painfully into the lintel. Using a choking man as a springboard, he flew above the ruckus and danced from table to table, kicking drinks into the crowd and showering them in their own alcohol. The man with the phone tried to get down in a panic and slipped. Virgil was on him in an instant. He raised a fist. The man's eyes went like egg-whites and he offered up the phone immediately. Virgil crushed it in one hand and sprinkled the pieces onto the man's midriff.

Stalking out of the pub, there were two more lummoxes drunk enough to get in his way. Virgil smashed a man's pint glass on his own forehead. Then roundhouse-kicked a huge biker over the bar and into the mirror lined with spirits. At the door, he turned back and pointed at Damian, who sat, huddled in a corner.

'TELL YOUR FRIENDS I'M COMING.'

CHAPTER TWENTY-SEVEN

THE RAM

'The town of Oldley, just a stone's throw from Derbyshire's jewel in the crown: the famous hill-village of Prestley, and a ten-minute drive from the Spindles; the Peak District's most distinctive rocks. Not perhaps, a place you might equate with explosive violence.

However, this traditional country town has, in recent years, become a haven for members of a controversial organisation. Against Radical Islam have grown to be one of the country's most popular right-wing groups, with marches having already taken place on the outskirts of Newcastle and Liverpool and another planned for Leicester. The movement's leader, Mark Wragg, explained to BBC News that there is a method in the madness.'

'We're trying to wake up these sleepy country dwellers and say, "your village church will be replaced with a mosque if you don't get your act together!'

'In the past, ARI have been linked with a number of violent protests, including the riot in Lincoln town centre which resulted in the tragic death of Police officer, Carol Dinkley, three years ago. Today, however, there was a very different end to the story.

At two fifteen, an undercover officer inside the Joiner's Arms made this phone call:'

'There's a fight by the bar, I can't see from where I'm standing but it looks like there's a black kid getting beaten up. He's wearing some kind of mask. Yeah, yeah, they're destroying him. Request all units to move in.'

'A truly chilling statement. When officers stationed outside attempted to enter, they were stopped by a large crowd, who blocked the doors with picnic tables and fought to defend the pub. But what was really going on inside the Joiner's Arms? BBC News has exclusive interviews with some of the ARI supporters who were there when the fighting started. The following content contains footage that some viewers may find upsetting.'

'He came in and everyone was laughing like, y'know this one guy acting like he could take us all, and then... well, I've got two black eyes and a fractured pelvis. The kid just laid into everyone.'

'It was almost like he couldn't be hurt. I know that sounds crazy, and yes, I have been drinking since nine, but the boy, he was black, real skinny, not a shred of fat on him, but there he was in the bar taking down guys three times his size.'

'He tried to hit me with a bottle. But I managed to duck and he only got my hand.'

'He had a sheep mask, like a Derby ram. Scary mate, scary…'

'A total of fifty-eight ARI members were taken to hospital with broken bones amongst other injuries. Five men had to be air-lifted to Nottingham for life-saving surgery. Among the more bizarre aspects of this story is the most puzzling detail of all—the insistence of every eye-witness that this was the work of one man.'

Virgil muted the TV. They had watched the drone footage seven or eight times already. It showed Virgil exiting the Joiner's Arms through the front doors, axe-kicking a guy off the picnic tables then laying waste to about twenty others who jumped him from behind the police van.

Pidge had posted the footage online anonymously.

The internet was ablaze with people analysing the clip, making all kinds of declarations as to the identity of the masked man. People were calling him *'The Ram'*. It was an incredible feeling. And although he hadn't planned for his first outing to receive such publicity, Virgil was glad of the message it sent: no-one was beyond the reach of justice.

~ ~ ~

Virgil had been checking the news for updates roughly every hour for the last two days. The description hadn't changed: **'Police have identified the suspect as being a black male between the ages of eighteen and twenty-five.'** He was especially pleased that they had misjudged his age, he just hoped forensics didn't turn up any DNA. *I guess, normally, I'd have been bleeding all over the place.*

On the Saturday night, he got two voicemails. The first had been from Mrs Crabble, offering to pay him to tidy up Floyd Burlock's garden. *'It is an awful eye-sore, I haven't been able to ignore it since you pointed it out.'* The second voicemail was more concerning. It was exceptionally brief and the Pastor's voice sounded strained.

'Virgil, Jerome here. Call me back as soon as you get this.' Virgil hadn't called him back. *What if he knows about the crypt? About Goldie? I can't give her back yet, not when I'm just getting started!*

He skipped church on Sunday morning, feigning sickness. When his mum returned, she said nothing about the Pastor. This worried Virgil even more. It was Monday morning, the final week of the Summer holidays. The days ahead sparkled with opportunity: Lawns to mow by day and a village to protect by night.

Had Virgil possessed the superpower of foresight, he might have stopped there.

CHAPTER TWENTY-EIGHT

A HIDDEN DOOR

Most vigilantes worked at night—Virgil knew that. But it made sense to get cracking during daylight hours. After all, this was August, so it wasn't getting dark until late. When he had done the lawns, he would text Pidge, who usually finished his butchers' job at a similar time. They would eat lunch, agree on a patch to patrol, then work in tandem, using the drone to watch for people in need. By now, their combined earnings had more than paid for the walkie-talkie earpieces.

Despite a bombastic start. The Ram's first few street patrols turned out to be quite dull. There was a lot of hanging about, then walking on to see if anything less-boring was happening around the block. He did rescue a cat from a large tree. And on the Wednesday afternoon, he broke up a scuffle at the cricket club. People stared a lot and the mask was terribly claustrophobic, but he felt so alive he barely noticed. A handful of times people made immediate 999 calls. Virgil ran away the first couple of times. But the third time, he refused to budge and the police were unable to move him. After he had snapped two pairs of handcuffs with ease, the officers backed off looking stumped and radioed their superior.

'I'm on your side!' he shouted after them.

Virgil decided it would be good to spread the sightings out. He and Pidge did a stint in Oldley, then asked Trent to drop them in Derby on the Thursday night. This too proved uneventful, unless you counted buying sandwiches for homeless people and clearing up sick outside nightclubs. Just as he and Pidge were preparing to go home, some drunks outside of Trance Bar challenged Virgil to a fight. In the end, he stood still while they broke their hands on him and their girlfriends cackled and cawed.

~   ~   ~

Friday dawned dry and bright, with a dusty skirmishing wind. He was due to mow Floyd Burlock's lawns later that day and had agreed with Pidge to meet there at eleven. But at nine o'clock, Pidge phoned, his voice was quivery and he spat the words out so low and fast that it was all Virgil could do to keep up.

'Pidge, slow down, mate. What did you say happened?'

'A dawn raid. Noise like a bomb going off. Opened my eyes and there's armed police, all in black, dragging me out of bed.'

'What were they doing? Oh... Trent?'

'Brought dogs in, took all his gear, I mean, even I don't know *all* the places he had it hidden but they were here three hours or more. Me, Dad and Chrissy sat on the sofa together in our underwear while they turned the house upside down.'

'And Trent?'

'Cuffed and put in a van. They said he'd either be charged or back tomorrow.'

'What do you think will happen?'

Pidge gave a mirthless chuckle, 'He's toast.'

'I'm sorry it happened the way it did, Pidge, sorry for you that is.'

'It's fine, Trent knew the risks. Anyway, I'm calling to say I won't be coming to help at Burlock's. I need to be here for Dad. Chrissy's been screeching at him non-stop and I'm worried he'll snap if I'm not around.'

'Completely understand. Call me if you need help.'

'Will do. Let me know if you find anything.'

'Laters, Daniel Dorker.'

'See you, Krav Maggot.'

~   ~   ~

Floyd Burlock's garden was far worse than Virgil remembered. Rocks, dead branches and an overspill of vines prevented him from mowing the lawns straight away. He made sure to knock on the front door and wait before he started work, but it was clear that no one had lived here for some time.

Did they ever send a bobby over to check on him? Or was I fobbed off?

Four hours later, he had cut both lawns and was standing inside the green bin trying to squash it all down. He hopped nimbly out and went to pack up the mower. He had only planned to peek through the windows, but curiosity got the better of him. Finding the back door locked, he was able to work a rain-damaged window open.

Checking the neighbours' fences to make sure he was unobserved, he slipped inside.

The house smelled musty. The place had a thin layer of dust on it, but Floyd was by no means a messy bachelor; everything had its own place; neatly organised—if a little seventies. Some grotesque ceramic dogs in human poses adorned the mantelpiece in the lounge, and the expected smattering of awkward family photographs lined the walls. *Nothing recent though. Wonder if old Pinky has fallen out with the fam...*

The entire house was clear. Virgil kept expecting to find a body or a stash of stolen cash. The only thing out of the ordinary was the apparent vanishing of homeowner and dog, *he always had that dog with him.*

On his way out, he noticed a crescent scuff on the stained oak of the hall floor. He followed the mark up to a door he had missed. It was wallpapered over and merged with the brown and pink stripes perfectly. There was no handle. Virgil gave it a nudge with his shoulder. There was a mechanical click and the jamb popped open. Fumbling the torch on his phone, he cautiously stepped inside. It was a box room, probably stitched onto the garage. The walls were a murky turquoise. It stood in such stark contrast to the rest of the house that it made his skin prickle. There was a desk. Upon this desk sat reams and reams of paper, all written on in the same untidy hand. Block capitals and un-joined. *Same as the note from his hat.* It was on the walls too—like the ravings of some cell-bound lunatic. Virgil moved his torch around the room. The cuttings and clippings climbed onto the ceiling like a black and white creeper.

Virgil felt an uncontrollable urge to rush out of there. He could almost visualise the unsmiling man, bowed over the desk, scribbling away, cackling from time to time. Unable to take it all in, he photographed all four walls and the ceiling. There was an open diary, which he slipped into the pocket of his cargo shorts. Scratched into the cover and inlaid with gold ink were the words: *The Full Armour of God.* That was all Virgil could take. He closed the hidden door with a springy click and returned to the freshness of the cut grass.

Halfway home, he realised that he had not called at Mrs Crabble's for payment. His head was bursting with theories, it was all he could do to keep the mower on the pavement. *What is Floyd doing cutting out all that stuff from newspapers? Why were there so many photographs of St Justus?* Virgil was itching to pore over the diary. It wasn't like him to steal it, *but,* he reasoned, *Floyd could be in trouble and this might lead me to him. Yeah, keep telling yourself that, thief.*

All these thoughts screeched to a halt, along with the wheels of a grey estate. It was Pastor Jerome.

'Put your lawnmower in the boot and get in.'

Virgil didn't need telling twice.

CHAPTER TWENTY-NINE

ARCHAEOLOGY

'**H**ow long have you had it?' Jerome stirred the teapot. Virgil fiddled with the frayed seam of the tablecloth. The old man turned, steaming spoon in hand. 'How long?'

Virgil took a deep gulp of air and blew it back out defeatedly. 'Since the start of the holidays.' He took Goldie off and laid her on the table. 'I'm sorry, I don't know why I took it.'

Jerome put the lid on the pot and poured out two mugs. He carried them to the table, then picked up the shield strap, turning it delicately. Then, to Virgil's great surprise, he slid the shimmering trophy back. Virgil sat there with Goldie in his lap, not knowing what to say.

'Keep it,' Jerome said. 'The martyrs only choose those who are worthy to wield the armour of God.'

'The what now?' Floyd's diary seemed to grow heavier in Virgil's pocket.

Jerome didn't speak for a very long time, he just paced the kitchen, stroking Luther absentmindedly every time he passed. Virgil waited patiently, it stood to reason that the silence was deliberate. Eventually, the old Pastor sat down and took a long draught of tea.

'I knew it was you even from the radio; an indestructible man. The Ram! It's catchy. Why the sheep mask?'

'I like it. It was Gramps''

'Mmm. I called your mobile.'

'Yeah… sorry for not calling back. I just didn't want—'

'To lose the best chance you've had at making a difference?'

'Er… yeah. Yeah, I've… I suppose I've always had an overdeveloped sense of justice but an underdeveloped physique.'

'There's no such thing as an overdeveloped sense of justice,' said Jerome. 'As MLK Junior said, "The time is always right to do what is right."'

'Sounds wise,' Virgil conceded. 'In reality, I've *felt* like that a lot, but always lacked the muscle to back it up.'

'Weak but worthy. What did you make of the martyrs' crypt?'

'Dark. Damp. Don't get me wrong, it's impressive in there, the statues and stuff, really amazing.'

'Do you understand now why there are such strict rules about access to St Justus—why every tour is overseen within an inch of its life by yours truly?'

Virgil spoke hesitantly, still putting it all together, 'You're protecting the crypt. And the artefacts inside.'

Jerome nodded solemnly. 'Virgil, what do you think our military would do if they knew St Clavius' shield grip existed?'

Virgil shrugged. 'I guess they'd want to take a look.'

'The Government would seize St Justus, weaponize every last piece of armour and sell their secrets internationally to the highest bidder.'

Virgil gave an involuntary shiver.

'How much do you know about St Justus?' Jerome had a twinkle back in his eye.

Virgil paused, not wishing to offend, 'Actually, Pastor, not very much.'

'You mean you find my lectures boring?' The twinkle shone brighter.

After a short pause, he said, 'I'm teasing. My historical lectures *are* boring. And it's just as well you've paid no attention—as they are full of inaccuracies and misdirection. We can't have some bigshot American archaeologist discovering the final resting place of the Israelite six. I distract them with the stars in the ceiling by taking them up the bell tower for nice views and tall stories about St Justus.'

'How do you know so much?' said Virgil. 'Who taught you about the crypt?'

'The only reason I know what I know is thanks to Margaery.' Jerome wandered over to the Welsh dresser and picked up a photograph of his wife. She had a beautiful heart-shaped face with a wide smile and dark twinkling eyes much like his own. 'Marge was an archaeologist.' He passed the picture to Virgil. 'She specialised in ancient middle-eastern poetry, among other things, and many of her digs during the early years of our marriage were based around Jerusalem.' He looked meaningfully at Virgil, encouraging him to put it all together.

'So, it was your Margaery who discovered the six saints.'

'She did, in their homeland, Israel. And once she was sure of their final destination, we *had* to come to England. I was already the Pastor of an independent church in the Holy City. With a few letters to the right people, I was considered for the position of Vicar here. It was the perfect ruse for Marge to conduct her work. That was twenty-five years ago.

Marge devoted most of her life to studying the Six and their impact on Prestley. She was a good mother, she poured all her considerable energies into charity work and representing the vulnerable. She chaired the Women's Institute too. But whenever she wasn't wife-ing or mothering or churching, she would be down in the crypt, dusting away at the ancient slabs, furthering her research.'

Virgil decided to broach the question he'd been itching to ask all week.

'Who is Floyd Burlock?'

The reaction on Jerome's face was instantaneous. A shadow seemed to warp his kind features, a contortion of unbridled rage. It was gone as quickly as it had come, but it left Virgil feeling hot and wishing he had kept his mouth shut.

The Pastor got up and began to pace, his fingers did a delicate little dance as he moved around the room. 'The information I tell you now does not *ever* leave this room. Understood?'

'Understood. I didn't mean to pry, it's just, someone mentioned him the other day in connection with the church and—'

'Floyd Burlock.' Jerome interrupted, 'Worked with Margaery in Israel. He was a lab technician at the Israeli School of Archaeology. They were not on speaking terms, but Marge would often confide in me that Floyd made her feel uncomfortable. He would… lurk when she was alone in the lab. Once she came back for her coat and found him rifling through her research papers. When we moved to Prestley, we thought we had left him behind. And for ten happy years, it was true.

Then, one Sunday morning, I step up into the pulpit and who should be sat at the back, but…'

'Floyd Burlock.'

'My sermon vanished clean out of my head. Margaery was inconsolable over lunch. I decided to pay him a *pastoral* visit. After all, sitting in my congregation, he was under my care. When I got to his house on Chancel Street, Floyd ordered me off his property, claiming never to have met Marge and threatening to call the police if I didn't stop harassing him.

It was very difficult. Every Sunday he was there, sitting in the same pew. He never spoke to us, never acknowledged our attempts to make friendly conversation, nothing. The worst part was that towards the other families in church, Floyd was the most wonderful extrovert. Because of the attention he showered upon everyone else, none of the clergy took my concerns about him seriously. He was only cold towards myself and Marge. Even our own sons thought he was delightful.

Happening parallel to this was a breakthrough in Margaery's research. She finally gained access to the inner crypt—by tunnelling through the Manse basement. And as she witnessed the power of the artefacts, she realised the need for utmost secrecy. Marge became convinced that Burlock had come to cash in on her success, and set about guarding the crypt both day and night. It affected her so severely that she stopped coming to services and then… and then…' Jerome wiped his eyes with the back of his hand. 'I used to have to take a plate of warmed-up dinner down to the crypt, crawling with it on my hands and knees just to see my own wife.'

'And Burlock?' Virgil's tea was untouched, 'Did he find the crypt?'

'The powers that be appointed him church gardener. That was the final straw for Marge; it tipped her over the edge. He would cut the grass in the graveyard and spend the rest of his time loafing around the grounds, sneaking down to the faux crypt whenever he could. Marge was convinced he was getting closer to discovering the hidden door.

Then, one night, I rolled over to discover her gone. I took a torch down into the sepulchre, but when she was not there, I began to panic. I drove into the village and got to her in the nick of time. She had broken into Floyd's house and was screaming at him in the living room. Then it happened.' Jerome swallowed. His leathery hands were shaking, so he gripped the table edge to stop them.

'There in Burlock's living room, she collapsed. My Margaery, in that despicable man's house. A stroke brought on by high blood pressure—like a seizure. Of course, the ambulance came to the house and people talked. What was the Pastor's wife doing at Floyd Burlock's place in the early hours? Floyd himself did nothing to deny the rumours. She was never the same from that day onwards, my lovely Marge.

I was miserable. I took a sabbatical. Lost the plot. I wanted revenge. For my boys who had lost their mother, for Marge, who had lost her dignity. The night we sent her to Felicity Gardens, I got drunk and wandered down into the crypt. I put on all of the armour, all six pieces. Then I phoned Burlock and invited him up to the graveyard, promising to spill St Justus' secrets in return for his signed confession: the affair was a lie.

It was midnight. September. I remember the cherry tree creaking while I waited. Burlock showed up in a trench coat and that dark side of the moon t-shirt he wears. He came towards me actually smiling, hand extended as if to shake on our deal. He thought he'd won. And so, I... I... at first, I didn't know what I had done.

You see, one of the artefacts I was wearing was the belt of truth. The wearer of the belt is able to make their adversary believe whatever truth they see fit. As Burlock came at me grinning, I just wanted him to disappear. I thought I might hurt him if he came too close. I willed him to walk away, to forget all about the crypt and the six. Go home and leave us in peace.'

'And he did,' whispered Virgil.

'And he did.' Jerome swung his hands together, 'Never came back. Not once. When church members visited, he didn't recognise them anymore. Didn't even know he was the gardener. The belt of truth had changed what was true for him.'

Virgil decided not to share Floyd's diary with Jerome. *Not yet.*

'I can't believe I have just told you all that,' Jerome admitted, 'I trust you, Virgil. You're a good lad. And it seems right that you have Clavius' shield, or the strap at least! You could do some real good with it.'

The two of them stood up at the same time, skirting the table, and embraced.

'I'm so sorry,' Virgil muffled into the Pastor's shoulder. 'About Margaery.'

'Psalm thirty-four, verse eighteen.' Jerome smiled through glassy eyes, 'The Lord is close to the broken-hearted and saves those who are crushed in spirit. Now, come on, let's get you home. I've got a long drive ahead of me this evening. I'm off to Leeds.'

'Jackson's birthday?'

'He's thirty-five tomorrow. I'm taking his favourite: flapjack. Want some?'

CHAPTER THIRTY

DEAR DIARY

Virgil wolfed his tea, thanked his mum, helped her into bed to do her catheter, washed up, warmed Maisie's bedtime milk, then carefully unwrapped the flapjack Jerome had sent him home with. He made coffee and took a generous stack to his bedroom. Floyd Burlock's diary banged heavily against his thigh as he walked. Once inside, he wedged a slipper under the door and sat at his desk. Pulling the stolen ledger from his cargo pocket, he laid it face-up on the wood. Marmalade light seeped through the curtains, glinting off the sunken lettering.

He opened the cover. A great wedge of notes had been torn out—the whole first half of the diary, leaving row upon row of frayed stubs. He snapped on the desk lamp and took a steadying sip of coffee. It hit the back of the throat with a comforting burn. Smoothing out the first unmolested page, he began to read.

25ᵗʰ Feb

'Why do I feel like I've done this before? The Full Armour of God. Those words, this diary... it all seems so familiar to me. Yet there is nothing I can tie it to. No person, no place. All I have to go on is a feeling, a vague, hard to define gut-wrench that tells me this journal with its missing pages was once important to me.

I was a gardener, up at the Church. St Justus. Though I have no recollection of labouring there. People tell me they know me. I used to "go for dinner". They say I lived in Israel once. I recall the heat and the stone. The Jews with their big hats, metal detectors, the taste of freshly-pressed oranges, the smell of butchers' shop blood running down the street. I recall every feeling, every sensation—but what I was doing there? Not a clue.

People avoid me. They whisper. One old crone was bold enough to tell me why. Apparently, before my amnesia, I was once a vibrant member of this little community. Can you believe it? Me! A mover shaker! That was until I had an affair with the Pastor's wife. I have seen pictures. I do not know the woman. Yet I am supposed to have driven her mad with guilt, or so the villagers say. It's hard to feel guilty for something you don't remember doing.'

Virgil flicked on a few pages. There was a drawing of the crypt doors.

'For years I have walked Jasper around Prestley aimlessly. Until today, I found my feet taking a different path. I followed them and arrived in the graveyard under the cherry tree that overshadows these doors.

I find myself drawn to the crypt. Its silence frightens me, even as it calls to me. There is something within, something I used to understand. Something terrible happened to me here, beside the cherry tree. What is the Full Armour of God? What made me scratch these words in gold on the front of you? Who am I? Who on earth AM I?'

Here, the page was blotted with ink and punctured with stab marks as if the pen had been driven into the page again and again. Overleaf, Burlock's ponderings resumed with detailed sketches of St Justus and the graveyard. There were runes and accurate recreations of the stained-glass windows. There was even an annotated breakdown of the grounds and Widow's Peak. Burlock was a talented draughtsman, whatever his morals. *Where did you go, Floyd?*

Not much happened for pages, just more drawings. It seemed that Floyd left the house every afternoon at 3.33 PM and walked to the churchyard. *That's why I would see him in the cut-through—he was on his way to the crypt!*

As he munched the flapjack and read the increasingly crazed scribblings, Virgil began to sympathise with the old man. It must have been infuriating to have had all those memories erased. Then he recalled the Pastor's tears while describing Margaery's descent. His sympathy turned to steam. He flicked to where the diary abruptly ended.

14ᵗʰ June

'I have cracked it. The first tomb is a façade. A hidden opening leads on. I go tonight. Jasper shall accompany me as before. He is a faithful mutt, but will doubtless be of little use against her. She is devilish. Foiling my plans even now. She found it but won't share it. I must do this thing. I cannot continue to live in the shadow of St Justus. Everywhere I go I am taunted by its piercing spire. This village, this hateful little village and its hateful little people. I am done with this place. The flat in Tenby is ready, but curiosity begs me to stay. What is in the crypt? I must know. I shall know. I shall know by nightfall.

I will destroy her. She found it but won't share it. Unlimited power lives within the crypt.

Report back when I return. Wish me luck.'

But Floyd never had reported back. The diary was empty from here on. The fourteenth of June. The night his white fishing hat had gone bobbing past. *He had gone to break into the crypt.* A chilling thought suddenly occurred to Virgil: *That heavy breathing, those shuffling steps... Could it have been Burlock? What if he's been trapped down there all this time?* Time and again, he had trudged up to those vine-locked doors. Then on his final visit, he had gone but not returned! Virgil thumbed back in time, scouring the yellowed pages for anything that might shed more light. Just when he was ready to give up, his finger landed on a phrase. *'Something terrible happened to me here, beside the cherry tree.'*

A stone dropped into Virgil's stomach as if from a great height. *The cherry tree.* A glimpse of flattened grass came to him. It was getting late but there was only one thing for it.

'Muuuum?'

Zelda's voice came back from the bedroom, 'Yes, darling?'

'Are you OK to sort yourself and Maisie out tonight? I'm going over to Ben's.'

'That's fine, if you could just come and kill this spider first, he's been sat in the corner watching me.'

~   ~   ~

Riding one-handed, he spoke quickly and in an undertone.

'Pidge, I've had an idea about Burlock.'

'An idea?'

'Yes. How quickly can you get to St Justus?'

There was a yawning silence on the line.

'Pidge, are you alright?'

'It's... it's just what's happened with Trent. I've not been good, mate.'

'Pidge, I was forgetting, sorry. I was so excited about this Burlock thing.'

'Think you know where he is?'

'I... maybe. It's a hunch, but I want someone with me.'

Another lengthy pause, then:

'I'll be there as quick as I can.'

They arrived at the same time. Virgil from the front gate, swallowing coppery spit and regretting every last piece of flapjack, and Pidge from the far gate near the Manse. Pidge's hair was wet and bits of his pale blue shirt stuck to him in dark patches. 'Shower,' he explained gruffly. They walked their bikes to the cherry tree and Virgil filled Pidge in on the afternoon's revelations.

'Does Jerome know about Burlock's diary?' Pidge gave a wet patch a futile brush.

'I decided not to tell him. He was so worked up talking about Marge, I thought it would tip him over the edge.'

Pidge perched on a lopsided headstone. It struck Virgil that he looked different, his eyes were bloodshot and he kept one hand in his pocket, fidgeting away at nothing.

'Pidge, are you Ok?'

'Yeah, mate, yeah.' Pidge gave a strained grin, forcing himself to look up and his fingers to briefly cease their machinations. Then he seemed to get a grip on himself. 'I'm fine,' he looked back down, straightening out his damp shirt. 'Home has been... Dad's been out of work, best part of a year, and we relied on Trent's cash flow to pay the rent... so we're likely gonna have to move out soon.' He gave a resigned huff. 'House is stressing me out. Chrissy's stomping around in hysterics. Dad's off the wall, drunk. I put another hole in my bedroom wall... pretty rubbish day all told.' Pidge massaged his collar. 'It's good to have something else to, to, to, to do.'

'And Trent?'

'Hasn't left his room. Awaiting the trial. They're processing the evidence.'

They sat together, comfortably, in the gentle evening heat. The sky behind Pidge was a ruddy blush of purple, candy floss clouds liberally scattered.

He looked to Virgil and said, 'So, what are we up here for? You said there was a clue in the diary?'

Beside the cherry tree.

Virgil faced the knotted trunk. The setting sun nestled somewhere within its low branches, blood-red, its gory rays filtering through the twisted fingers. His shoulders slumped; he realised he had been putting it off. It was time to investigate. A dull prophetic doom beat inside his heart, he knew that whatever they found next would put an end to their Summer daydream—the dynamic duo. He got onto his hands and knees and began to crawl towards the tree.

CHAPTER THIRTY-ONE

UNDER THE CHERRY TREE

'Virgil, what're you doing?'

'I have a theory about the grass.'

'Grass you've been smoking?'

'No, this grass under the tree, it's all pressed down like there was something lying here, like there—'

Virgil recoiled with an inward shriek. His hand had touched something cold. Cold and fleshy. It hovered above the flattened turf, in mid-air, completely invisible to the naked eye.

'What is it?'

'It's a—' he reached out with both hands now, 'It's a—' Getting a grip on the material, running his hands until a palm brushed metal. 'It's a body.'

Pidge was by his side, 'Are you having me on? There's nothing there. Look.' He planted his foot where Virgil guessed the head must be. When it connected with a wet thump, Pidge drew back almost to the bikes. 'What *is* that? You don't think...?'

Virgil held the shoulders and shook. 'Mr Burlock? Floyd? We're here to help.' He stopped. The skin under the shirt was clammy like raw chicken, the old boy had been dead some time. Probably since the fourteenth of June. It was only then that he noticed the smell and the flies that fizzed around the felled mass—an invisible banquet. He ran his hand along the shirt collar and found metal again. Closing his fingers around what felt like a handle, he stood up, still gripping. It slid out easily, and the body appeared suddenly at his feet. Facedown in the long grass.

'ARGH!' Shouted Pidge. 'VIRGIL! Where'd you go? What the? What the?'

Virgil stared at the knife in his hand. Congealed blood had dried onto the hilt. The blade was gloopy with it. His eyes went in and out of focus from the trembling gold dagger to the dark slit in Floyd's neck, and back to the dagger.

'Virgil! VIR-GIL!' screamed Pidge, hollering into the whole graveyard. Virgil snapped out of his reverie and threw the knife down on the grass.

'SHHH! Stop shouting or you'll bring the whole village up here!'

Upon Virgil's reappearance, Pidge nearly fell backwards over the bikes. 'You were gone! It's, it's, it's...' his voice trailed off, processing. 'It's that knife, it's another magic artefact, isn't it?'

'It must be,' said Virgil, almost too shocked to move.

They stared at it, a golden blade lying innocuously amongst rippling green ones. If not for Floyd's blood, it might have been a thing of beauty. Virgil's mind was doing gymnastics. 'Pidge, you realise how this looks?' Their eyes met. '*I* informed the police when Burlock went missing. *I* took them his bloodstained hat. And now, here *I* am "discovering" the body two months later in exactly the same spot! My DNA is all over him, my prints are on the murder weapon—'

'If it *was* murder.'

'Are you kidding?! Look at his throat! Do you really think he did that to himself?'

Pidge's head see-sawed, his hand was in his shirt pocket again, fidgeting away. His cheekbones looked more sunken than ever in the twilight. His legs swayed and his body twitched, but he was fixated on the knife. It suddenly dawned on Virgil that his friend was high. *He's not thinking straight.*

'Pidge?' he said tentatively.

'Hmm?' Pidge's eyes didn't leave the blade.

'You weren't in the shower, were you? You splashed that water on yourself to try and sober up.'

'Don't judge, Virge. I've not used Trent's gear in ages.' He side-stepped closer to the knife. 'The police thought they'd confiscated it all, but they didn't check Chrissy's car.'

'OK, but, Pidge. Pidge!' Virgil clicked his fingers, 'Pidge, what are you thinking?'

'I'm thinking you've got Goldie. Makes you invincible, right?'

'So?'

'So, this golden dagger makes the holder...'

'Or their victim—'

'Invisible.' They said in unison.

Pidge's hand was out of his pocket, the fingers worked over each other like the legs of a pale spider.

Slowly, he lifted his gaze to meet Virgil's. The two friends connected with laser intensity.

All the oxygen seemed to suck out of the graveyard.

They dived for the knife.

Pidge had been standing closer and disappeared as soon as he hit the ground. From where he lay with a handful of grass, Virgil saw the tell-tale impressions as his friend went from prone to standing.

'Pidge!'

'It's nothing personal, Virgil!'

'Pidge!'

'I can't speak to the fuzz, I'm stoned as a skunk! I need the knife. And no murder weapon puts you in the clear too, right?'

'Pidge, don't do this! You're not thinking straight! Ben?'

There was only silence.

Virgil got up and ran his hands over his head. He should never have invited Pidge up here. Was it coke Trent sold? That stuff was supposed to make you paranoid. *No time to sit and sulk. There's a body with my prints all over it and a case file which specifically names me as the last person to see Burlock alive.*

Things looked bad. The worst bit was—he had absolutely no idea what to do next. He couldn't call Jerome for help—*he will be in Leeds by now, anyway. What if he's the killer?* He wasn't prepared to hide the body. He called out to the clouds in silent desperation. In the windswept quiet that followed, words of wisdom filled the aching void. It was Gramps, years back, his brow was wrinkled mahogany, a finger wagged: *'Be sure your sins will find you out.'*

This murder wasn't my sin. So, I'll be found innocent. Right? Right?

He looked at the body more closely. Floyd's right arm was outstretched where he had fallen. Some animal had nibbled at the knuckles, stripping them to the bone. Virgil shuddered. Burlock's neck was purple and bloated, swollen to twice its usual size. His face ate grass. But for the backs of his ears, his head could have been one great grey pineapple. Aside from the single entry wound, there didn't appear to be any other sign of injury. Virgil forced himself to look closer at the feasted-on hand. Clutched within its cage of fingers was a handful of wiry, black hair, shot through with grey. *Not unlike Jerome's.*

Had the memory wipe worn off? Had Burlock started returning to this spot until the Pastor cracked? Virgil withdrew from the sickly putrefying odour and opened his phone. Before he dialled, he noted that Pidge's bike had disappeared. *He must have taken it while I was examining the body.* Virgil allowed himself a wry smile, imagining the turquoise mountain bike riding itself back home.

He dialled 999.

'Hello? Hello... Police... I'd like to report a murder.'

CHAPTER THIRTY-TWO

CRYING WOLF

Virgil stumbled into St Justus' foyer in a daze. He reckoned on having minutes before blue lights swarmed the hilltop. On the TV, suspects were strip-searched and deprived of all their belongings. He *had* to hide Goldie before that happened.

His feet made a lonely tapping on the chequered tiles. Coming to the south transept, he searched desperately for a hiding place. In the cool of the still, stone cloisters, the panic subsided. Virgil gave himself a moment to drink it all in, perhaps for the last time. How he had failed to appreciate the beauty of St Justus week after week! It seemed cruel to have so little time left to enjoy it. There they were, the six saints, each immortalised in their own stained-glass window, tinted crimson by the dusky sky. For the first time, Virgil realised that Ephesians 6 was quoted beneath, the old letters hammered into the limestone: *belt of truth, breastplate of righteousness, shoes of the Gospel, shield of faith, helmet of salvation, sword of the spirit.* Turning back towards the entrance, he let his eyes follow the star-strewn ceiling which hanged above the nave. The stars twinkled, channelling the dying sun, a million droplets of crystalline claret poised to plummet. At the far end of the ceiling was the round rosary window, which filled much of the south wall. Virgil had always thought it depicted Golgotha, but now that he looked, the hill with the skull face was clearly Widow's Peak and there were six crosses atop its precipitous edge.

Six protectors, six vigilantes. Virgil wondered how it had played out for them. Had St Clavius and St Ingrid spent their nights pacing the streets, waiting for something to happen?

Sirens in the distance. Getting closer. *Snap out of it! You've got to find somewhere NOW!* He skidded over to the baptismal font and lifted the wooden lid. Wrenching Goldie off his arm with a grimace, he bunged her inside, dropping the lid with an echoing clunk. *We aren't due any christenings, she should be safe. She had better be safe.*

Back outside, he waited by the noticeboard, stepping back as the panda cars crunched gravel. Two officers approached while the others held back. He recognised the one who spoke first, it was the dimple-chinned man with the coffee stain from Oldley Police Station. James Siddons. He had shaved today.

'You called it in?' Siddons' tone was calm, matter-of-fact. As if working a murder case in Prestley was business as usual.

Virgil gulped and nodded. 'Follow me,' he said, in a voice which sounded like an adolescent Kermit the frog. He led them through the gate, towards the cherry tree, feeling like the world's most macabre tour guide. *And on our right, ladies and gentlemen, my latest victim.* The panicky voice in his head chuntered away as he forced his feet onward, towards Floyd Burlock's piebald neck, towards the flies. Virgil had never seen a dead body before today. He braced himself for a repeat viewing.

It was gone. The body was gone. There was no blood, no flattened grass—it had all been ruffled back up to standing. There it swayed and billowed in the breeze, mocking him. Virgil stood dumbfounded, with his hands at his side. The policemen gave each other a look.

'Where's this stiff then?'

'It was here. He was right here. I swear, I—' Virgil got down on all fours, scrabbling around the patch where Floyd had lain. There were still a few flies around. 'Take some swabs!' He looked up to the officers who both had their arms folded, looks of annoyance and consternation splashed generously across their faces. 'You'll find his DNA all over this bit of grass!'

One of the officers walked off, radioing as she went.

'It's a hoax. Some village idiot seeing things in the graveyard.'

'IT'S NOT A HOAX!' Virgil called after her. James Siddons remained, arms still folded. 'Did you follow it up?' Virgil asked, 'The hat with the blood spatter?'

Siddons shook his head. 'The force is stretched at the moment.'

'I found his body. Here. A gold knife sticking out of it.'

Siddons' lip curled sardonically, 'You found the body in the *exact same place* as the hat? But eight, nine weeks later? He had just been lying here in plain sight, all this time? Don't take us for fools, son. You know the one about the boy who cried wolf.' Siddons pulled what he clearly thought was a disappointed face, 'Look, I'm going to get back in the car now and we'll say no more about this little incident. But waste our time again and it'll be a formal warning. Maybe even a criminal record.'

Virgil's arms gave out, slumping onto his knees.

'Take care, McAllister. Get yourself home. And stop hanging around this graveyard. Go down the park, buy an Xbox, do something *normal* kids do.'

Virgil wasn't listening. Part of him was filled with relief at not being the prime suspect in Floyd Burlock's murder trial. Part of him was worrying about what Pidge might be doing with the knife. *Did he move the body?* As Siddons' sweat-drenched shirt departed, Virgil's overriding thought was one of disappointment: If the police hadn't followed up Floyd's hat, there was no way they were still looking for the Saxo lads.

Before leaving, he slipped back inside the church and retrieved Goldie. He had felt strange without her, vulnerable again, alive even.

~ ~ ~

The weekend was an interwoven patchwork of lawn-mowing and caring for his mum, who thought she had the beginnings of a pressure sore. Months of unbroken scorching had rendered the majority of Prestley's lawns yellow and bare. Only the most committed villagers had managed to keep theirs green. Despite the heat, Virgil made sure to do his best—edging every drop off with care and tying prize flowers away from his blades. The people of Prestley tipped.

He hadn't seen or heard from Pidge since Friday night. The knife was undoubtedly the implement which had kept Burlock's corpse hidden all this time. It was also, for someone like Ben Pidgeon, a godsend. As he mowed stripes into another vast lawn, Virgil pictured his friend scoffing Post Office pick and mix free of charge. *Don't be silly, Pidge has changed, he's no petty thief.*

Sunday morning rolled a warm breeze over the village. On a bed-bound Zelda's insistence, Virgil took Maisie to church and was relieved to find that Jerome was away, still in Leeds—Virgil verified this. Upon reflection, he welcomed the evidence that Jerome couldn't have moved Floyd's body. *Maybe he isn't involved at all.* The day passed. Still nothing from Pidge.

Bank holiday Monday evaporated in a final blaze of heat and Tuesday awoke to overcast skies. Clouds pregnant with long-awaited rain lined up on the horizon, vast and grey and boiling. Virgil tied Goldie loosely around his thigh and reluctantly pulled on his school uniform.

CHAPTER THIRTY-THREE

KNIVES OUT

The first day of term was remarkably uneventful. Virgil kept himself to himself. In Pidge's absence, there was practically a queue of people wanting to sit next to him on the journey home. *Since when did I become popular?* In the crush for the bus, a chess clubber called Emmet Frog attached himself like a limpet and claimed the spare seat with obvious delight. Virgil nodded vaguely as Frog yammered on about coding all the way home. Pretending to look in his rucksack, he saw that Pidge had finally replied to his texts.

'Had some stuff to sort out. Will explain soon. Promise.'

'OK. I can't believe you left me with Burlock!'

'I know, I'm sorry. What happened with Burlock in the end?'

'You didn't move the body?'

'What? No!'

'We need to meet face to face. You can keep the knife. I just want my wingman back.'

'Give me 48 hours. Tying up some loose ends.'

Exactly what this meant, Virgil would have to wait and see. He hoped Pidge's 'loose ends' were more ambitious than spying on Georgia Higham getting undressed, but less ambitious than robbing a bank.

Daniel Dauber had returned to Bulwark with a new haircut but the same old scowl. He had not approached Virgil at all today, and avoided eye contact in the lunch hall. Smiling and nodding at whatever Frog was saying, Virgil swivelled in his seat and canvassed the back of the bus. Dauber's crew were subdued, and Big Boss himself slumped out of sight, the only thing visible were his frosted blonde spikes. Virgil tuned into Frog who was still blithering on:

'Nobody believed it at first, but then Jamie Creighton posted the video and wow, I mean wow, Virgil. You taking down Daniel Dauber. Just wow.'

So that's why I'm suddenly popular. 'Did Jamie get the bit where I ran off and wet myself?'

'He, erm, no he didn't. Erm, that's a joke, right?'

'Excuse me, Emmet.' Virgil stood.

He started down the bus, making for the back seats. As he went, his fingers scrabbled around the bottom of his bag until they found the smooth glass encasing June Dauber. He had brought the picture to school with the intention of returning it to Daniel. *I should never have taken it.* Everyone stopped what they were doing to watch. No one approached the back seats, not without leaving a will.

Virgil held the photograph close to his chest. All the back-seaters looked dumbly at it. Keegan Rice nudged Dauber.

'Deej.'

He looked up, and, seeing the image, rose quickly and snatched it away, burying it in his jumper. His eyes flickered upwards fleetingly. They looked weary; all their venom was gone. Virgil shirked his bag back onto his shoulder and Dauber actually flinched.

Virgil leaned on a headrest, 'I'm sorry about what happened in the bathroom,' he said, 'I should never have stamped on your ribs. And I'm even more sorry for taking that photograph. From what I've heard, your mum was an amazing person.' He lingered, unsure if he had connected at all, but he thought he saw Dauber's reflection nod. The once towering kickboxer held the jumper tightly around himself and refused to acknowledge those friends who urged him to get up and flatten the imposter. Feeling there was nothing more to be said, Virgil made his way back to Emmet Frog.

~   ~   ~

Virgil was going crazy sitting at home, waiting for the rain to come. His imagination was working overtime, wondering what Pidge might be up to. *Might as well do a patrol,* he thought, *kill some time.*

At nine o'clock, he caught the bus to Oldley. LAW-N-ORDER had given him pockets full of spare change— it was nice not to cycle the back roads for once. Goldie exerted a reassuring pressure on his thigh, and in his backpack, the Ram waited.

'The Derbyshire Ram, patrolling the streets of Oldley,' he muttered in his gravelliest voice, 'bringing justice to the oppressed, one head butt at a time.'

'Whaddid you say?' said an old drunk on the adjacent seat.

'Oh, nothing, go back to sleep.'

The clouds broke at nine-thirty. Great fat globs splatted the aching streets until they became a neon mirror. As people dashed past, holding their coats and umbrellas against the downpour, Virgil felt reborn. The rain was invigorating.

At ten, he helped move some café tables indoors at O'Reilly's Irish Pub, then sat with homeless Brad Finnegan for a while, chatting about videogames. Brad was awfully forgetful and kept asking about the mask.

'It protects my secret identity,' Virgil repeated for the millionth time. It never stopped sounding cool. He bought Brad a sandwich from the pub, then continued his patrol.

Around eleven, he was walking down a leafy avenue called Featherfield when the backfiring of engines burned the soaking air. Four motorbikes came buzzing down the residential street towards him. Their leader pulled a wheelie. Curtains twitched and a woman appeared in the amber glow. Virgil gave her a thumbs up, then stepped into the road. The bikes saw him and u-turned.

They pulled up in a semi-circle, blocking his path. The leader—whose sodden tracksuit was grey, with white stripes running the length of his arms and legs—pulled off his helmet and spat on the ground very close to Virgil's feet.

'What are you supposed to be? Halloween is next month.'

'Actually, it's still August, so two months away.' Virgil scratched his chin under the mask. He should probably leave these bikers to it. But it had been a quiet night. The other three took their helmets off. Virgil prodded the lead man's chest, 'I hope you asked your sister's permission to borrow her pyjamas.'

His face dropped and he revved his engine.

One of the others said, 'Do him, Paul.'

Virgil held out his hand, 'Nice to meet you, Paul.'

Paul rocked the throttle and came straight at him, but Virgil stepped neatly out of the way. The back tyre sent a spray of rainwater six feet into the air as the bike squealed a doughnut at the other end of the street, then came racing back at a phenomenal speed. This time, Virgil didn't move.

Paul tried to readjust at the last second, but the tyres aquaplaned. The bike split in two over Virgil's shins. Its rider was thrown spinning into a drain still bubbling with overflow from the long-awaited deluge. Turning over the wreckage with his foot, Virgil wondered whether this was the stolen green Yamaha from Spotted Oldley. He took a photograph on his phone, then began to walk off.

'Call your friend an ambulance! And get him some new pyjamas!'

Tell-tale splashes, three pairs of running feet. Helmets back on. Metal flashed in the yellow streetlights. Virgil turned back and caught a wrist as it was driven down towards his temple. From the side, another slashed at his intestines. Knives. He hated knives.

He broke the first guy's wrist with one rotation of his hand. Then grabbed the second knife by the blade and rocketed its handle right through the coward's visor. The helmets muffled their surprise as the two of them staggered about in the pattering rain. Deep thunder rumbled overhead. The third helmet put his knife carefully back in its sheath. Virgil held out his hand. The youth wisely obeyed, handing the weapon over. Virgil saw the Ram mask reflected in the visor. *So cool.*

'SCRAM!' Virgil yelled. He had never told anyone to scram before, he didn't even know the word was in his vocabulary.

It worked.

Virgil was dog-tired and soaked—time to clock off. The Ram had taken three knives off the streets. That was probably enough for one night. He sat at the back of the bus, daydreaming about different ways he could disarmed the riders. When he arrived home, drenched and trembling, Virgil didn't notice that his bedroom window was open wider than he had left it. He slunk inside and was sitting on the bed pulling off his socks when a voice whispered,

'Alright, Krav Maggot. You're home early!'

'Pidge! Man alive!' Virgil put a hand on his heart, 'You scared the pants off me!'

'Socks by the look of it.'

'Where are you?'

A clunk, as Pidge laid the knife on the desk, simultaneously appearing in the armchair.

'Sorry I've been gone so long,' he whispered, 'but boy, have I got a story for you.'

CHAPTER THIRTY-FOUR

GHOSTS

'First of all, I owe you an apology. I realise that was a really rubbish situation to leave you in with the body and stuff. I can't believe someone shifted it while you were gone! Must have been a relief?'

'I can't describe it. You know, I honestly saw myself getting locked up. They took one look and assumed it was a hoax.'

'But who could have moved him? Your Vicar?'

'He's out of town, visiting family in Leeds.'

'Hmm.' Pidge itched his crotch. 'Well, it wasn't me. When we found the body, it was like I could hear the sirens all around us. It's why I grabbed the knife with both hands! Some friend I am.'

'You're a brilliant friend. Everyone makes mistakes.'

Pidge looked across the bedroom, a smile caught at the corners of his mouth. 'Thanks, mate.' He came over and sat next to Virgil, making the mattress bounce. Pulling out his phone, he brought up his camera roll. 'Time to explain myself. My week as Mr Invisible...' He swiped to a photograph of an empty cabinet. 'This is the evidence room at Derbyshire Central Police Station. And *probably* the only illegal thing I did this weekend...' When Virgil gave him a quizzical look, he burst out, 'I removed all of the drugs they seized at Trent's arrest!'

'Ben,' said Virgil, 'if we're going to be protectors, we have to uphold the law wherever we can. Not use these powers to exploit the system.'

'I know, I know. But he's my brother. You've met him, Trent's a good guy, he deserves a second chance. I promise I won't do anything like it again. But that's not all. After I abandoned you, I felt awful. I wanted to find a way to make it up to you.' He slid a crumpled post-it-note from out of his wallet. 'Do you know what's on the same floor as the evidence room at Derby Central?' Virgil shook his head. Pidge's face was triumphant, 'Archives, my friend, archives.'

He passed over the post-it. 'This is what took me so long. I couldn't always get in, and I had no idea how the filing system worked at first, but... open it.'

Hands trembling, Virgil slowly unfolded the piece of paper. Jotted, in Pidge's untidy hand, were seven words. He swallowed them, and they pooled in his stomach cold and foreign.

TREVOR LEE

13 VASSAL ROAD,

MICKLEOVER,

DERBYSHIRE,

DE3 5HG

Pidge said solemnly, 'I know what I would do if it had been *my* mother.' He cast a lingering look at the dagger on the desk, then climbed out of the window.

~   ~   ~

Virgil wasn't sure how long he had been standing there, but the clock said eleven. His feet were freezing as he clambered into bed. He tucked the address safely in the sock drawer. Not that he needed it, the words were branded on his brain with a hot iron. All those feelings came gushing back: the resentment, the burning, biting, bitterness. Oh, the revenge he could have—between Goldie and the dagger—and no one would ever know! Was there a higher power? Someone up in the clouds watching? Or had Karma just handed him what he was owed? All he knew was that Louise was taking his mum into hospital tomorrow to get her bedsore looked at. They would be gone all morning, with her little red Corsa left sitting on the drive. It was too perfect. He couldn't have planned it better. Dark fantasies gave way to dark dreams, only this time, there was a twist. It was no longer Trevor Lee who stalked Virgil through his nightmares, now Virgil was stalking *him.*

~ ~ ~

'I can't sorry,' said Tony, 'I have a prior commitment, I'd love to have her, I really would. But it's something important and I can't miss it. Have you asked Pam and Mick?'

'Ooh! Good idea, they got back from holiday yesterday. Thanks, Dad, see you around.'

'See you around, chum. Have a good d—'

Virgil put the phone down and called Pam. A minute or two later, he was thanking her profusely and passing her Maisie's bag. This was happening, it was happening this morning or never at all. He didn't feel he could go through with it if it were even a day later. He was in the zone. He was in the vein. It wouldn't be pleasant, but it needed doing. *For justice's sake.*

He kissed Maisie and waited for Pam to retreat back into the house. Then he quickly unlocked the Corsa, bunged his rucksack in the passenger seat and started her up. As he backed Zelda's car off the drive, he prayed that Pam hadn't come back to the door, and that nosey Diane at number seventy-one wasn't curtain-twitching this early on a Saturday.

It took thirty-four minutes to reach Mickleover. Virgil would have preferred to have the radio on, or even better, some thrash metal to keep him fired up. But he found it too hard to concentrate on the Sat Nav. This was, after all, the very first time he had driven on a public road. *Thank goodness Mum drives an automatic.*

He had fastened Goldie extra tightly today, knowing what lay ahead, and left the knife resting in the drinks holder in case he needed to vanish at short notice. Once he was away from roads he recognised, he relaxed. No one who saw him now would think, 'What's that fifteen-year-old doing driving?'

As he pulled onto Vassal Road, Virgil was holding onto the wheel as tightly as he could. His hands were slick with sweat; it had even run into his eyes, making them itch and sting. Wanting to distance himself from any form of witness identification, he parked two streets away. Donning a pair of latex gloves, he picked up the dagger and began to walk.

As he approached the house, Virgil's heart was reverberating inside his chest so fast that he felt like some man inside his ribcage was giving the longest drumroll of his career. The street was full of tired-looking town-houses. Number thirteen had a van outside it on bricks, and the porch window was boarded up. He opened the gate carefully and squeezed through, avoiding the tangle of creepers strewn across the front path. In front of the door, he took a deep breath, then knocked.

All he's going to see is an empty step. Then I... then I... But what was he going to do? Straight up murder this guy? What if someone else came to the door? *If someone else answers, I'll slip past them and we'll go from there.*

None of these questions mattered as the house remained static—no answer. Virgil pulled his fist back and punched the lock. The door frame splintered and two panels hung out. He gave it a more accurate blow and the handle and Yale-lock landed heavily on the bottom of the stairs. He stepped inside and waited. Nothing. *He's either out or asleep. I'll sweep the downstairs first.*

He went into the kitchen. The place was a mess. There were dishes on the rack as if someone had started washing up but then lost interest. Every other surface was covered in bottles. There were short brown ones and long green ones. There were two-litre cider bottles and one-litre vodkas. There were just about as many different types of bottle as Virgil had ever seen. The only thing that united them was that they were all empty. Out in the yard, he could see more bottles peeking out of the overflowing recycling bin and another two bin bags filled with what were presumably more bottles.

Looks like dear old Trev didn't kick his alcoholism then. Virgil let the dormant anger begin to boil up within him. How irresponsible! How unthinking! Maybe he would have been pacified to arrive and find Trevor Lee had turned it all around and was now a charity worker or a missionary. But to find him still entrenched in alcohol abuse—the very thing that had robbed Mum of her legs... well... He tightened his grip on the knife. *He deserves this.* He poked his head into a grimy downstairs bathroom, nothing. But coming into the lounge, he sensed it, there was someone in there.

A stained red armchair squatted in the corner. On it lounged a malnourished ghoul. Lee was almost unrecognisable from that little black and white photograph two years ago. Virgil had to get closer to make sure it was him. But yes, those eyes; too close together; that mouth which hung down at the corners; the slightly inbred look his wonky ears gave him. This was him all right. Virgil didn't know what to do now. Lee was just sitting there, gazing vacantly at nothing. There were empty bottles on the carpet and another clutched in the blackened nails of his left hand. His skin was so thin, it looked as if it might flake off. Only his blinking and the faint rise and fall of his chest made him more than a corpse.

Virgil took two steps towards him, the knife felt unbearably heavy. He reckoned that even if he were visible, Lee would remain staring at the smoke-yellowed wallpaper. He positioned the blade above the heart. One push would do it. One push and then all he had to do was walk away.

He braced his arm. Moving his feet apart in case there was any splashing. *Am I really going through with this? Am I really going to wipe out such a pitiful excuse for life?*

Virgil thought of his mum struggling across the garden to get to Maisie. His mum crying in the night when she thought he couldn't hear her. He thought of all the things she couldn't do, and all the things she now *had* to do because of this man, his carelessness, his selfishness.

He let the pain consume him, relegating all rational thought to a lockbox in the back of his mind.

He moved to thrust the knife in.

CHAPTER THIRTY-FIVE

A BETTER WAY

The blade would not slide in. Virgil felt sick, he pressed harder but his own inhibitions stopped the point a hair's breadth away from penetration. *You could stop now, walk away,* Virgil's whole body was vibrating, *you don't have to do this,* his grip on the handle faltered as the first trickle of blood ran down Lee's bony ribs. It wasn't the knife though, Virgil realised that his own nose was bleeding. The sight of it shocked him. *Let go. You're not a killer.*

'Daddy?'

The voice made him leap out of his skin. He spun around so quickly, he slipped on a bottle and came crashing down on the hearth. The little girl was standing in the doorway clutching a dirty-looking rabbit teddy and sucking her thumb. She had dark curly hair which spilled onto her shoulders, and her eyes were darker still. She couldn't have been much older than Maisie. Her pink t-shirt read 'born this cute'. She wasn't looking at him, Virgil saw with relief that his white-knuckled hand still held the knife.

'Daddy, you OK?' the girl came trotting up to Lee, who remained catatonic. 'Daddy, look! Bloods! Daddy cutted hisself!' The little girl clambered into Lee's lap and started to dab haphazardly at the trickle. Her fat hand massaged the blood into Lee's chest until it looked like a bad case of sunburn. It was hard for Virgil to tell though, as his tears ran freely. He pinched his nose with his free hand, eager not to drip on the carpet. The girl and her father became two watery blobs which rippled and swam in front of him as he fought to control his breathing.

He managed to get to his feet. The little girl had curled up on her father's chest. Virgil wanted to go over and stroke her curly locks the way he stroked Maisie's, to thank her for stopping him. Had he killed Lee, there would have been no returning to the person he was before. His own conscience would have hounded him forever. *Murderer.* He took a deep draught of the fetid nicotine-air and blew it out slowly, weighing up his next move. *I've got to get out of here.*

Carefully re-entering the hallway, he stopped and listened. Footsteps. Someone was coming up the garden path. The door swung open on its hinges, banging into the pile of dog-eared shoes. Virgil threw himself against the wall and inhaled so quickly he almost choked. Standing there, wearing hole-ridden jeans and a rugged baseball cap was... *Dad?*

Tony McAllister stepped into the house, dropped the bags of food and examined the broken door.

A horrible thought dripped into Virgil's mind. What if his dad had somehow got the address and was coming to finish what his son started? What if he was dressed like this to kill?

Then Tony called out, 'Tabby? Tabby, darling, you mustn't run ahead like that!' Virgil drew back, awestruck. *He brought the girl.* He let his father pass, then followed him into the lounge. 'Tabitha!' Tony scolded, 'I said, you mustn't run ahead like that! I was still getting the shopping out.'

'Uncle Tony!' she leapt off Lee's inert kneecaps and ran to him, 'Daddy done cutted hisself!'

'Trev?' he moved quickly to the alcoholic's side, leaning over him and checking his pulse. 'Your door is all smashed in and—how did you?' He scanned the floor for sharp implements. Then got on his hands and knees and felt for broken glass. 'Tabby, I think we had better put your shoes back on until we find what Daddy's cut himself with.' He searched Lee's chest again, 'Can't see a cut... come on, Trev, let's get you up and dressed. CAP starts in an hour.'

Virgil watched his father for the next hour, collecting all the empty bottles, tidying, cleaning and generally organising Lee's squalid house. He stuck CBeebies on for Tabitha, then helped Lee strip off and get into the shower himself. The drunkard was coming around now, and with a little prompting, was able to dry and dress himself.

'Careful on those stairs!' Tony shouted up from where he sat at the kitchen table, sorting through Lee's post. When the freshly-washed Trevor staggered through the door, Tony held up two piles. 'OK, this lot is mostly advertising, so we'll recycle that, and these are your bills and important bits. I paid your council tax this month.'

To Virgil's surprise, Lee's eyelids squelched a few times and then he cleared his throat and spoke, 'Thank you, Tone. Don'tknowwhaddi'ddo without you.' He coughed drily onto his fist.

Thirty minutes later, they were at the village hall and Tony was speaking to Lee again in the same patient, slow voice,

'Remember, Trev, no one is going to judge you. Everyone is here to help each other. It's Christians Against Poverty now in the hall and then Alcoholics Anonymous straight after. I'll take Tabitha to the park and collect you when we're done.'

Virgil watched the man of his nightmares shake his dad's hand and push through the double doors. He looked shrunken. He was greeted by a smiling blonde woman with a name badge. Much to his own surprise, Virgil found himself willing Lee to do it, to break the cycle. He watched him disappear through the doors. Feeling somehow lighter, he trotted after Tony and the pushchair. Quickening his step so that he was right behind his father, Virgil pocketed the knife.

'Dad,' he said.

Tony jumped and turned around.

'Virgil? What're you? Oh, no. I know how this looks, but it's not how it looks. I haven't got a secret family, what's happened is—'

'Dad, I know.' Virgil crashed into his father, pulling him into a bear hug. 'I know about Trevor Lee. How you've been helping him.'

Tony's body loosened as he prised his son off. 'How did you find out?'

'I came to his house,' Virgil swallowed, 'I was going to, you know… revenge.'

Tony's face softened, 'Of course.'

'But when it came to it. I, er...'

'Couldn't go through with it.?'

'Yeah.'

Tony ran a hand under his cap. 'Same thing happened to me.' He stared blindly at the pharmacy opposite. Tabitha groused restlessly in the buggy. 'Let's walk and talk.

I came here just over a year ago. Found out the prisoner release date, showed up with a baseball bat. I broke in just fine, but in the end, I couldn't bring myself to do it. The idea of hurting him had kept me going so long, but by the time I had him at my mercy, more suffering didn't seem like the answer. There had to be a better way, I thought. So, I used my connections in social work, started to try and help him instead.'

'Does Mum know?'

'I don't think so. I mean, she knew about me coming here. Tried to convince me to spare him. Your mum wanted us to forgive Trevor from the beginning, just like that! Forgive the guy who'd ruined her life! It was one of the things we argued about most. It has taken me a lot longer to make my peace with the situation. But in reality, being a part of Trev's rehabilitation has been the perfect antidote.'

'How's he getting on?'

'It's slow for sure. But there have been improvements. He's almost quit smoking, and although he still drinks a lot, he is cutting down.'

'I do think it's great, Dad, really I do. It's just... well, I think you know what I'm going to say...'

'It seems weird me giving Trevor all this support while you struggle at home with Mum.'

Virgil looked at the tarmac.

'Yeah.' Tony sighed mournfully. 'Yeah, it's a tricky one. This might not make sense to you now, but, at the same time as I started helping Trevor sort himself out, your mother was being particularly difficult. She is wonderful. But she's also very driven, self-sufficient. Always has been. It's one of her greatest strengths. But it made her very difficult to help. Your mum was doing a lot of self-processing and I felt like I wasn't needed. I began to pour all my energies into fixing Trevor instead, and your mother and I just grew... distant.'

'Mum doesn't need fixing, Dad. She needs loving.'

They arrived at the park. Tabitha squirmed to be let out of her harness and when Tony unclipped her, she made a beeline for the swings.

'And Tabitha's mum is?'

'Absent. She left Tabby with Trevor the weekend he got out of prison. Of course, social services quickly spirited her away. But I have made a point of bringing her to visit, heck of a lot of paperwork, but I think it could be the thing that helps him conquer his demons.'

'Uh-huh. And Trevor… does he know who *you* are?'

'Yes. I told him early on. We don't talk about it though; makes him drink more. For the meantime, we are just old friends.'

Virgil stayed with his dad for another hour talking about Zelda. By the end of it, Tony was tearful.

'Don't phone now,' Virgil advised, 'She's at the hospital.'

'I need to come home. You really think she would have me back?'

'I know she needs *someone*. And you made the vows.'

They said their goodbyes and Virgil sprinted back to the car. He managed to shave five minutes off the drive home. He collected Maisie and was sinking into the sofa with a strawberry milkshake just as Louise and Zelda pulled up.

He tried to make his face normal, as if today he *hadn't* almost become a murderer, as if the Corsa's bonnet *wasn't* red hot.

He pondered it all—these golden items that invited violence. The futility of revenge. Most of all, he pondered his dad's game-changing realisation: There had to be a better way.

CHAPTER THIRTY-SIX
FILLING UP

September morphed into October. The mornings bristled with a chill air and the nights were drawing in. Brooding banks of pewter-grey cloud became a permanent feature of Prestley's skyline. For the first time in eons, Virgil felt hopeful. Zelda's pressure sore had turned out to be a bad bruise, she supposed she had done it transferring into the car. Either way, her relief was tangible, and although he didn't show it, Virgil also breathed freely again. The idea that his night-time escapades might have put his mum back in hospital curled his toes.

Tony had started calling around for tea. Once a week at first, but now regularly. And from the muffled conversations he caught, Virgil thought things between his parents were improving. They had even hugged on the drive last time and he danced Maisie around the lounge so fast that Zelda scolded him when she returned.

Jerome resumed his duties at St Justus, but he wasn't the same. Even half-asleep on the front row, Virgil could tell that his sermon lacked oomph. His eye didn't twinkle and his hands stayed glued to the lectern. As for the little white foam that would appear at the corner of his mouth when he really got going... *I have never seen his lips so unfoamy.* Jerome was polite on the door, if a bit cold, he asked about school. Virgil mumbled something about it being better this term, to which the Pastor nodded sagely. He clapped Virgil on the back and moved him on, shaking the hand of the next sheep.

Out in the graveyard, Virgil wandered over to the crypt. Thick planks of wood had been hammered over the entrance with yellow and black tape tacked haphazardly across. A sign read, **Condemned. Do not enter.** He pulled at a flapping piece while he waited for Zelda and Maisie. Why was Jerome so distant after all the secret conversations they'd had? *Why is he pretending like we don't have a connection?* It was as if the Pastor had left his personality in Leeds. Virgil wanted to go over for scones and tea again. To ask Jerome outright about the body. *'Floyd Burlock, Pastor, lying in the exact same place you wiped his memories!'*

Weeks passed. The invitation never came, Jerome kept on pretending and Virgil got the hump. Some Sundays it was like the elderly Pastor had forgotten his name. *Maybe he doesn't think I've got what it takes. Maybe he's disappointed in me.*

October was rolling to a close, with Virgil and Pidge engrossed in their studies. Both had been off school with heavy colds and had a lot of catching up to do. As a result, they were reluctant to go out at night. The last time had been an absolute snooze-fest—no action, nobody misbehaving, just aching cold feet and the feeling they were wasting their time. Virgil found himself willing something to happen, wanting an argument to break out or a car to swerve dangerously. He would strain his ears for raised voices, then hail Pidge,

'Anything from the skies?'

'Nope. Everyone's in bed.'

Prestley was a sleepy village. Why hadn't he realised it before? Maybe he had been too engrossed in the power fantasy to see that he wasn't needed here. He began to understand why fictional heroes protected whole cities.

For Halloween, the duo made plans to go to Derby. They would catch the eight o'clock bus from Oldley station and be in the city by ten to nine. Surely there would be problems to solve on All Hallow's Eve. Shedloads of other masked madmen to put down.

Since his weekend of invisible antics, Pidge had sworn off the knife. He claimed it had scared him, taken him places he 'wouldn't normally have gone'. The blade remained in Virgil's care, he started to keep it in a padlocked box in the sock drawer. With his history of sleepwalking, he wasn't taking any chances.

~   ~   ~

The X51 was early and the two friends boarded, gratefully handing over their fares. As St Frederick's Bus Station shrank in the large wing mirrors, they sat with bated breath, both imagining the night that awaited them. Pidge checked the batteries in the drone's remote, then checked them again. The bus was nearly empty. A couple of girls in devil's horns whispered coyly behind them. Pidge zipped up his bag and sniffed up some post-flu phlegm.

'So, Virge, I've been thinking... Virgil?'

Virgil had not replied because he was staring out of the window. The bus was stopped at a junction on the north-east of Oldley, just before the A7 hit countryside. A TEXOIL petrol station took up the corner, diagonally opposite a car-dealership, its red and black logo refracted in the dealership's polished exterior. There was a hunk of cobalt blue in amongst it all, which had caught Virgil's eye. As the bus began to pull off, he sprang across the aisle, pressing his nose against the grimy windows.

'Virgil? What's up?'

It was a blue Saxo all right, parked at the petrol station, and there were men inside. Young men. One of them was going inside to pay. The pattern on his arms was unmistakable, even at this distance. *Skulls.*

'Pidge, I'm so sorry,' Virgil called breathlessly as he pressed the emergency stop button and raced to the front of the moving vehicle.

'Hey! What's the big idea!' The driver rapped on the plastic divider, 'Next stop's a half-mile that way.' She flicked a doughy finger toward the fields.

'Open the door! I need to get out!'

'No!' She put her foot down and Virgil lost his balance, catching the rail just in time.

Pidge arrived, 'Are you feeling alright, mate? What's got into you?'

'No time to explain!' he machine-gunned the words out, 'Gotta go!' Virgil slipped Goldie onto his wrist and wrenched the folding doors apart. 'Thank you!' he shouted into the driver's apoplectic face. Then jumped, tumbling over and over on the scratchy asphalt and hitting something solid with a metallic THUNK. He got up and brushed himself off just as the lamppost came crashing down in a shower of sparks. 'Whoops.'

Running at full-pelt, he made for the TEXOIL sign. He kept his head still and his eyes always on the Saxo. The spindly trees on its periphery danced to the rhythm of his footfalls. At fifty feet, he slowed down and walked casually onto the floodlit forecourt. The Saxo was the only car there. Jones had left the music on; a deep undertow of bass vibrated the petrol-stained floor.

Virgil skirted the pumps, peering through the gap. There were two in the back. He couldn't see faces, but going on head shape, it was a dead cert. Damian and Kade Wurzel. Both held cigarettes. *Idiots.* He was leaning to get a better look at the front passenger seat when the shop door went and Patrick Jones swaggered out. He wore a tight black t-shirt which accentuated his gammon-joint arms. A hockey mask was pushed up onto his head. *So that's how it is. Any excuse to terrorise the neighbourhood.*

He slipped the backpack off his shoulder. Feeling for the zip, he reached inside for the Ram. Goldie slid off his left hand and onto the ground with a soft chink. But as he bent down for her, a beefy forearm tightened itself around his neck.

'Didn't think we'd be seeing you again.'

Virgil gasped for air as he was hoiked to his feet. He knew this arm. A crescent of scar tissue sat just out of focus. His own signature bite mark. He went to make another one.

'Ah-ah-ah! Not this time, you little rat!' Benjamin Gill twisted his chokehold so that Virgil's mouth was angled upwards. All he could see was the filthy underside of corrugated steel which sheltered them. He tried to speak but found he could only gurgle. If Gill squeezed any harder, that might become a permanent feature.

'Oi! Jonesy! C'mere!'

The driver's side door re-opened with a blast of grime, then slammed, dowsing the noise. Boot heels on concrete. Virgil scrunched his eyes shut and felt around the floor for Goldie. *If I can just slip her over my trainer…*

'What's this? A gold bracelet?' Patrick Jones' shoe scuffed Virgil's away as he knelt to pick her up. 'And a bag full of surprises! Ey up, Benji, I think I've found a new mask!'

Virgil screamed at the top of his lungs. His windpipe let out a pitiful hiss.

'Let him go, Benj,' Jones' voice took on a frightening quality. Virgil was suddenly free and his vision swung giddily as he spluttered his lungs onto the oil-film floor.

He tried to stand. Jones was wearing the Ram mask. His arms were folded. The skulls grinned from their thorny bed of vines. Doors banged. All four of them were out of the car now. Mist from the fields was creeping in, it drifted around their ankles in eddies of poisonous white.

'This is the one, Damian? The one from the Joiner's Arms?'

Damian didn't speak, he looked grey.

'Seriously. This is him? "Tell your friends I'm coming"?'

'Jonesy, you didn't see what he did to all those people. Look, mate,' Damian addressed Virgil directly now, coming forwards, a quivering wreck. 'We don't want trouble. If we give you back your bag, you can go and we can go and we'll—'

'Like hell we will!' Jones shoved Damian into the pumps, knocking a black snake from its holster. 'This bag is mine. Look! He's carrying around his mum's jewellery!'

'GIVE THAT BACK!' Virgil's voice echoed around the deserted forecourt. He could see to his right that the cashier was on the phone. If he could keep them talking until the police arrived...

'You thought you could scare us, but we don't scare easy. What have you been doing, following us all this time? Crusader for the disabled or something?'

'You owe my mum an apology.'

'And you owe your mum a trip to Sweden. Go put her out of her misery. Wheeling around like that. What kind of life is that?'

Virgil flew at him but was knocked on his bottom with ease. Jones was holding Goldie loosely in his hand. He checked his mouth. It felt as is every one of his teeth had punctured his top lip. The whole thing swelled up.

'Put him in the car,' Jones said.

'In the car?'

'Just do it.'

Benjamin Gill and Kade Wurzel grabbed him and started dragging. But Damian's clarion voice rang out,

'He's faking on you! He's faking! He'll bury you all! I've seen it! I've seen him do it!' He took off across the road, 'I'm calling the police.'

'Damian!'

'Leave him. I told you he couldn't hold his drink.'

Sharp fingers dug into the soft of Virgil's armpits as they lifted him. The toes of his trainers cut brief paths in the ground mist, coming to a halt outside the car. His head grazed the door as he was shoved roughly onto the backseats. Kade hotched over and pinned an arm across his chest, while Gill and Jones got in the front. Then the Saxo screeched off the forecourt, leaving portals of fog spiralling under the floodlights.

CHAPTER THIRTY-SEVEN

A CIRCLE

The needle fluctuated between eighty-five and ninety. Virgil was flattened against the seat as the Saxo accelerated. The car's horsepower was breath-taking, but Jones' handling betrayed him; he was no rally driver. His seat was so low that he strained to see above the wheel, and he braked *on* the bends—not before them. Virgil could feel his airway closing. Every second that passed with Kade's hand on his chest dragged like molasses. He was desperately conscious of his lack of seatbelt.

Jerking the wheel with a flourish, Jones went around some parked cars and drove on the wrong side until an oncoming truck forced him back. It gave a long blast on the horn as it thundered past. Neither Gill nor Kade seemed fazed—they were not wearing belts either. *They must be accustomed to this style of driving, or too cool to say otherwise.*

Goldie dangled from Jones' wrist, tantalisingly close as he made gear changes. He still wore the Ram mask.

'You sure you can see in that thing?' Gill's tone was jokey but his tight grip on the ceiling handle told a different story. *Maybe not so cool after all.*

'Fine,' grouched Jones. 'Makes me feel like a hero.'

'Where are we taking him?' said Kade, elbowing Virgil's chest as he adjusted in his seat. He stuck his head between the front seats. 'Devil's Den?'

'Where else?' Jones said in that dark voice again.

Virgil gulped down iron saliva from his smashed lips. Devil's Den was a popular haunt for teens. A secluded hollow which ate into a hillside not far from the Spindles. He thought of the mist which had flooded the forecourt. Not tonight, he couldn't go there tonight.

'Oooh, The Den!' Benjamin Gill rubbed his hands together. 'Haven't been there since, Jonesy's... *partay.*' Jones slapped the steering wheel, chortling. Kade, eager to join in, banged both headrests a little too hard.

'Stop it, Kade.'

Jones put a hand to the rear-view mirror, Virgil met his gaze with unflinching hatred. He wanted to speak. To tell the three of them to say their prayers. Instead, he said nothing. *First rule of Krav Maga: keep the element of surprise firmly on your side. Give your enemy no time for counter-preparations.* He cast a sideways glance at Kade, who had removed his restraining arm and was sulking, staring out of the window.

It had to happen now. They were only a couple of miles from Devil's Den. He closed his eyes to focus. The Saxo drifted on a sharp corner and Virgil's head hit the window. He rubbed it woozily. Kade snorted. Shaking his head then looking back outside.

Jones' snake eyes flashed in the rear-view again. 'Kade, why aren't you holding him?'

NOW!

Virgil swivelled on his back like a tortoise and kicked Kade hard in the chin. He went down in the footwell, clutching it. Wasting no time, Virgil swung a closed fist around Gill's headrest and caught him flat on the nose as he turned to see the commotion. Jones clawed backwards with his free hand but had to keep his attention on the few feet of road that the Saxo illuminated. Shrinking back into the corner, Virgil was able to avoid the arm as it thrashed, Goldie swinging off the wrist like a pendulum. *Got to pick my moment. Careful now. One blow from that hand could shatter my kneecap.*

Then, with a horrible stomach plunge, he froze. The seat in front: Gill was gone. *Well, he didn't open his door, so he must still be—*

'GAHHH!' Gill appeared briefly, his hand closed around the knife as he brought it out of Virgil's thigh and plunged it down again, this time scraping the top layer off his shin. Virgil felt dizzy. Nothing hurt yet, but there was blood on the ceiling, his blood. He could feel it running hot down his leg. It dripped on the handbrake where an invisible Gill held the knife.

'What the? Benji? Where'd he go?' Jones grabbed hold of Virgil's bleeding leg. 'What did you do to him?' He flung his attention back to the road, correcting the wheel just as it set their course for the undergrowth. Virgil didn't answer, he was watching the drips. Any second now, an invisible blade would come for him again. It did. But in a stroke of luck, Kade Wurzel threw himself on Virgil just as Gill brought the knife down. It disappeared, hilt-deep in Kade's shoulder. Then clattered onto the dash as it was yanked out again. Kade let out an unearthly yell and shuddered uncontrollably. Gill fell back, a hand slapped over his gaping mouth. Why Jones hadn't stopped the car yet, Virgil would never understand. The driver spun the wheel and called to his friend,

'Kade? Kadey?' The bloody dagger, slid across the dashboard, 'What have you DONE TO HIM?'

Jones abandoned the wheel altogether and lunged into the back. The Ram mask was knocked off his face. Kade's seeping shoulder rubbed dark patches onto Jones' t-shirt as he reached for Virgil, every finger a lethal weapon until...

With a cry of triumph, Virgil extricated Goldie from Jones' wrist. He shook her down his own arm until she nestled safely around a bicep. Then he went to work. Rolling Kade off, he smashed Jones' forehead with a palm thrust. Then he took one gammon-joint arm and threaded his free hand through the gap behind his elbow. He had never used Pidge's signature move on a real person, but now seemed as good a time as any. The car swerved but stayed on the road. The back of Gill's head was just visible as he gripped the wheel, one set of knuckles bone white, the other scarlet. Virgil looked deep into his enemy's convulsive face. He noted the freckles on high cheekbones, the startling blue eyes. Jones could have been handsome were his gums not pulled back over a crowd of teeth in feral pantomime.

'WHAT YOU DID TO MY MOTHER! SAY SORRY!'

Jones said nothing but held onto Virgil's jacket, both fists twisting the material. Virgil pulled on the elbow, bringing Jones' set of uneven teeth hissing to life. Then he fainted, slumping on top of Kade. The gammon-joint arm went limp, and slithered from Virgil's grasp, flopping down next to the mask.

Virgil wriggled out from under the dead weight and scrambled into the front. Benjamin Gill sat in the driver's seat. The car was teetering on the edge of control, but still, he kept his foot down.

'STOP THE CAR!' Virgil jabbed the meat of his arm.

'NO!'

'YOUR FRIENDS HAVE NO SEATBELTS. CRASH AT THIS SPEED AND IT'S ALL OVER.'

'IT'S ALL OVER ANYWAY! KADE'S DEAD.'

Fat tears ran down his face, he wiped them away and the Saxo veered onto the verge. Virgil grabbed for the wheel and then they were fighting over it. There was nothing Gill could do to stop him, Goldie saw to that, but still, he pushed the pedal to the floor. The needle leapt from ninety to one-hundred-and-ten. White and black arrows glimmered up ahead.

'TAKE YOUR FOOT OFF THE PEDAL, YOU IDIOT! YOU'LL KILL YOURSELF.'

'AND TAKE YOU WITH ME!'

Virgil tugged at Gill's right leg and managed to hold it up, then Goldie slid off his hand and he caught her just in time. Gill stamped back down and the Saxo burst forward again. The corner zoomed closer—they were nearly upon it. Then something stunned Virgil like a white-hot poker between the frontal lobes. There were lights; another car coming the other way. As they came into the bend, he fancied he saw her behind the dazzle of juddering headlights: a woman, her mouth a black hole of shock, and worse still, her baby strapped in the back. They were heading right for her, too fast to stop, inevitable, magnetic, destiny.

'NO!'

Virgil let go of the wheel and pulled the handbrake. The Saxo drastically altered its course, missing the woman by a whisker. It teetered on two wheels, still doing one hundred miles per hour, and then the dark horizon was the wrong way up and they saw stars through the windshield. Virgil fumbled with Goldie, desperately trying to fit her over Gill's hand too. But the inside of the car was spinning like a tumble dryer and he was weightless. The Saxo seemed to stay that way for several seconds. Over and over, caught in some terrible purgatory between the haunted trees and bottomless sky. Then it came down with the loudest bang he had ever heard. Everything caved in. Up was down. And silence.

CHAPTER THIRTY-EIGHT

VOICES

The lights in the Manse were on and Virgil could just make out the statuesque form of Luther in an upstairs window. He stole through the graveyard, wincing at the shooting pains in his thigh. Staggering over to the boarded-up crypt, he ripped away the metal sign. **Condemned.** The word pierced him. Placing his fingers through a gap, he tugged at a plank. It came away easily, the two nails which had held it jutting out like rusty fangs. He pulled at another, then another until there was an opening big enough to slink through. Then he took the knife out and held it gingerly. One final use, then never again. Goldie seemed to chafe more than usual, almost as if she was aware of his intentions.

As he plunged into the tarry blackness, visions floated in front of his eyes unbidden. Red tail lights on tree trunks.

The crinkling of misshapen metal as he dragged himself over a concertina bonnet. He pushed on. *Keep thinking about the car. Keep it to the car itself and you won't have to think about... them.*

He sat down in the darkness. He could smell petroleum, hear it leaking into the mud. In a blink, he was back in the Saxo. He craned his neck to survey the damage. The car roof looked like an elephant had sat on it. The only person who remained inside was Kade Wurzel. Whether the knife had killed him or the inverted door was unclear. The sight of his lifeless face sent Virgil scurrying.

The remaining headlamp shot a beam of white across furrowed ground. A bare foot caught that light. Benjamin Gill was lying spread-eagled, without a scratch on him, staring up at the stars. The impact had thrown him straight through the windshield. He was stone cold.

Patrick Jones was perhaps the most surprising of the three. How it could have happened, Virgil had no idea. But Jones hung from the limbs of an oak tree, two or three metres above the hedgerow they had cleared. His arms dangled together, still moving as the branches bent and groaned. All of him was red, whether from the brake lights or something else, Virgil didn't look closer.

Police had been on the scene fairly quickly. But by then, Virgil was three fields away. There was no way he was staying there with them—three corpses of his own making. Clutching the knife close to his chest, he had walked to a nearby road and called a taxi. The driver seemed to buy his story about a midnight walk gone wrong and dropped him at Oldley General. By the time law enforcement caught up, he had hidden Goldie, the knife and the Ram mask, and received seventeen stitches in his thigh.

When the police got to him, they reinforced that he wasn't in trouble. The footage from the TEXOIL garage put him in the clear. But the detectives wanted to know exactly what had transpired in the car. What had he been stabbed with? Where were they taking him? Virgil told the truth, mostly.

His mum and dad arrived together. Both were wide-eyed and too shell-shocked for tears. Zelda chastised him for approaching the Saxo but didn't lay it on too thick. No one wanted to suggest that Virgil might be responsible for what happened. Only, he was. *If I hadn't jumped off that bus, those three would still be breathing.* Forcing the last twenty-four hours out of his thoughts, he stood up and cracked his head on the damp stone of the passage ceiling.

'Ow!' he said out of habit—but Goldie had rendered it painless. He continued his journey downward.

He pushed the loose panel and the stone slid away to reveal the tomb of the six. The sepulchre looked as it had all those weeks ago. The solitary pinprick of light sent its heavenly ray down. And the saints lay obediently around its circle. Virgil forced the lid off St Clavius' sarcophagus. He was working on unfastening Goldie when a sound made him stop. There were voices somewhere out there in the darkness. Two voices.

Keeping Goldie on for the time being, he crept carefully in the direction of the sound. It was emanating from the third passageway; the one from which the shambling steps had come. *I have the knife this time,* whatever was up there would not see him. He padded up the tunnel. Unlike the other two passageways, this third one kept going straight and had no discernible incline. Then, suddenly, it took a right and Virgil arrived at a large circular door. The voices were louder now and he recognised one of them. *Jerome.*

The door was ajar and a sliver of light escaped, running along the floor and up the tunnel wall. He pushed his face gently against the opening—it was too small to get through. Hoping it wasn't a creaker, he pushed delicately at the panelling and stepped inside. The space within came as such a shock that he momentarily forgot his curiosity. The room was smaller than the tomb of the six but similarly shaped. The circular walls were lined with handsome mahogany bookshelves and the ceiling went up in a fresco which looked as if children had tried to recreate the stained glass from St Justus. Several workbenches filled the first part of the room, littered with an assortment of desiccated stonework and tools. The far side had a cosier feel, with two leather armchairs astride a magnificent woollen rug, and facing a roaring log fire.

Jerome stood by the mantelpiece, swilling a half-drunk glass of wine. There was someone sitting opposite him, a woman by the shape of her crossed legs. The two continued to talk, it was friendly, banterful. The kind a husband and wife might have over the dishes. *Wait a minute.* Virgil crossed the room like an arrow, ignoring the protest from his stitches. He rounded the second armchair, staring at its owner. A mass of wiry grey afro. A headband which kept the overhang off her high forehead and deep brown eyes. A bulbous little nose with a ring in it. And a mouth much like Jerome's, where the creases and wrinkles fell naturally toward laughter. Margaery Yeboah sipped at her own wine and twiddled her toes in the rug.

'Of course, you *want* to, but I won't allow it.' Margaery had a deliberate way of speaking; the left side of her face played catch up to the rest. 'He was all for the disturbance of other people's final resting places. It's fitting that his end is as dishonourable as theirs honourable.'

Jerome stared into the licking flames. 'But is it for us to decide, Marge? Granted, Floyd did everything in his power to destroy us, but doesn't it sink us lower to leave him unmarked? What about his—'

'Family?' snapped Marge, 'What about *our* family?' She gestured at the childish brushstrokes which covered the ceiling. 'Think of what he took from us. From me. No. This time, I decide what happens to him. I was never happy with him staying in Prestley. You know that.'

'But can't you rest now, dear? Perhaps this would be the perfect time to return to public life.'

'I...'

'The church would welcome you back. Times have changed, *people* have changed.'

'I still have work to do. There's so much we don't know about the precursors. And we're still waiting on Virgil.'

Jerome ran the rim of the wine glass along his bottom lip, 'You were so sure about him, I know it must be hard.'

'The jury is still out. Of all the candidates, Virgil has come closest to the six's original mandate. He understands anonymity, respects the armour, its pitfalls. It was his sense of right and wrong which singled him out. And the armour hasn't affected that. Remember, he called the police when they found Floyd. He knew he would be the prime suspect. But he called it in anyway.'

Jerome flashed his many white teeth, 'He still believes in justice.'

'And we should still believe in him.'

Husband and wife let the crackling logs take over for a while. Margaery closed her eyes. A black shape slunk through the crack in the door. It was Luther. The cat made straight for Virgil, then, to his horror, began nuzzling at his leg, licking at the dressing on his flayed shin. Before he could stop him, the moggy was winding his way in and out of his invisible legs. He crouched and desperately tried to shoo him away. Margaery was watching the cat with narrowed eyes. Jerome still had his back to him, he put his empty glass down.

'Why do you think he hasn't come back? I expected him to come looking for the rest of the armour.'

Margaery's eyes left the cat and looked straight at Virgil. He moved so that she was staring at where she thought his head would be. Still, the effect was unsettling. *She knows.*

'Perhaps,' she stroked a blue bead on her bracelet, 'he has broken the cycle. Perhaps he has managed to master the armour.'

'How long are you giving him?'

'Before I wipe his memory and take it all back?' Margaery shrugged, 'Ten days, a fortnight?' She yawned. 'Anyway, darling, you look done in. Go on up with Luther and I'll follow. I simply *must* finish this chapter.'

'Ok,' Jerome kissed his wife on the head as he left, scooping up the yowling cat. 'Don't be long.'

Margaery opened her novel and put the bookmark between dry lips, scrutinising the page. When she spoke, it made Virgil jump.

'Nice of you to drop in. I've been leaving that door ajar for weeks.'

CHAPTER THIRTY-NINE

THE SECRET SAINT

He laid the knife on the hearth, then stood self-consciously, waiting for Margaery to speak again. She gestured to the second chair. 'Sit.' He obeyed, the leather was impossibly comfy, but he didn't relax into it.

'Can I get you a drink?' Margaery inclined her head, 'Jerome keeps a stash of ginger beer down here. Has done ever since the boys were young.'

'Your sons knew about this place?'

'But of course! I spent most of my working life down here, beavering away at the dig. It wasn't until Floyd came knocking that we sealed it all up. I'd been here ten years by that point.' She took up her stick and made her way to a cupboard between the bookshelves. Her left foot dragged and she used only her right hand to retrieve a can and close the cupboard door. Virgil felt a swell of pity for her.

'You're wondering why I have stayed hidden away for so long.' Margaery loped back to her chair and sank in with a sigh, she passed him the can.

'Thanks. Well, yeah, it is quite a big surprise.'

'You were only young when it happened. I found myself in Burlock's front room, screaming at him. I didn't recall picking up the hammer but there it was in my hand, and then, this searing pain,' she touched the side of her head. 'I'd had a stroke. They whisked me off to Queens for an operation. Metal skull plate and all that.' She paused and took a long sip of wine. Virgil opened his ginger beer.

'But you're not...'

'Crazy? Unhinged? Wait 'til you've heard me out, kid. If you ask me, what I *was*... at first anyway... I was *hurt*. Deeply. These people I had adored, who I lived to serve, abandoned me at the drop of a hat. The rumour started—an affair with the parish gardener. It was up to my friends at the WI to shoot such salacious hearsay where it stood. But they didn't. It was too juicy. Too perfect. It made for such delicious gossip, and no doubt people used it to feel better about themselves. When I came out of rehab, there were more whisperings than welcome backs.

I made a decision to fake my own incarceration in some far-flung mental institution. What did they care?'

'Felicity Gardens,' said Virgil, 'Cornwall isn't *that* far away.'

'To the best of my knowledge, no one ever visited.'

'I'm so sorry.'

'Don't be,' she smiled. 'You were young. Anyway, I wasn't there, was I? My apparent absence gave me the perfect cover to stay in Prestley.'

'You never left?'

'Not once. Have you been upstairs in the Manse?' Virgil shook his head. Margaery continued, 'It's a big house. Couple of motion detectors carefully-placed. I always have time to hide. Plus, there was the sword of the Spirit.' She pointed at the hearth, where the flames made the knife edge wriggle and writhe. She winked. 'I have never missed one of Jerome's sermons. Who do you think sits in that empty front row?'

Virgil put down his ginger beer. 'I'm sorry, Mrs Yeboah, this is a lot to take in.'

'Call me Marge, and I'm not finished yet. You see, I want to shed some light on your relationship with St Justus. With the tomb of the Six, in particular.' Virgil sat up. 'That's right,' said Margaery. 'Didn't you think it strange that you found yourself drawn to the crypt, much in the way Floyd Burlock had been?' She brushed a hand over her baggy purple shirt, it lifted slightly and Virgil caught a glimpse of gold.

'The belt of truth,' he whispered.

'My weapon of choice,' she crooned. 'By far the most potent piece of armour. It even renders that knife obsolete—using the belt, I can convince your brain that it can't see me.' As if to demonstrate this, she laid a finger on the buckle and vanished. Popping back into view a second later with a titter.

'Is Jerome in on it?'

'Not a chance, I changed what was true for him first. I didn't want Jerome having to lie about me. It would be against his conscience. So, every time he leaves the house, I just… Poof!' she waved her hand, 'And Jerome believes I am still at Felicity Gardens. I even convince him that he pays me regular visits there. It's true for him, and saves any slip-ups. Then when I'm with him, I just reinsert the truth. He adjusts immediately like slipping on his favourite shoes. We've even entertained old friends for dinner. It is worth the look on their faces and all the kind words that come tumbling out. Even if I do have to expunge it all on the doorstep.' She sighed, 'I even sat in for your chats with Jerome. Who did you think baked those scones?'

'The flapjack too?'

Margaery flicked her eyebrows in the affirmative.

'What and you just wiped yourself from my memory?'

She smiled sadly, 'I had to make sure Jerome got it right. Said all the things I wanted to say to you.'

'Why on earth would you want to speak to me? We've never met!'

'True for you. But not for me. We have met many times, Virgil. Every time you *sleepwalked* up to the crypt. At my suggestion, of course.' She touched the belt again. 'Please, let me explain myself.'

'I think you had better.'

'When I came out of rehab, Jerome confessed to accidentally wiping Floyd's memory. He was ashamed, but I was ecstatic. A large part of my life, keeping St Justus' secret, was now over. What to do next? Jerome urged me to return to public life. But I saw the value in remaining at Felicity Gardens. For years, I had studied the Six. I wanted to honour their legacy by dealing out the same kind of justice they once had. Who would suspect me? I was in Cornwall.

I became Prestley's protector. Using the armour, I went about purging the village, then the surrounding towns. Did you know that Oldley boasts the lowest national crime rate?' She jabbed a thumb at herself, 'Me. In recent years, I found myself drawn to Bulwark Academy. I became a guardian angel for students who found themselves at the bottom of the pile. One of these was Joshua Brown.'

'Joshua?'

'Yes, Virgil, you weren't the first person to stick up for him. Though you were a great deal braver than me. I was invisible the whole time. Didn't you wonder why Joshua never got beaten up?'

'I had wondered.'

'That day you injured those two boys, I was off-duty. Jerome had a hospital appointment that I couldn't miss. When I found out about your exclusion, I felt terrible. Especially with you as my protégé.'

'Protégé?'

'What I mean is… I'm not getting any younger. The stroke makes getting around difficult at the best of times. You saw how I let Joshua down, and in time, I will fail others. It's time I passed the torch. I've been training you to take over. It is no coincidence that you have found yourself drawn to the Crypt. When you refused to come down of your own volition, I simply had that meat-head Daniel Dauber throw you in.'

Virgil snorted, 'Mrs Yeboah, this is insane—'

'I needed you to believe that the shield strap was your own discovery. It was the only way I could judge whether you were worthy of it.'

'Mrs Yeboah—'

'Marge, please.'

'Marge. You've got the wrong guy. I *do* care about injustice. Sometimes too much. I can't seem to let even the smallest thing go. But these artefacts... their powers... they have turned me into the very thing I despised. Three people are dead because of me.'

Margaery squeaked leather, 'I had wondered if that car accident had anything to do with you.'

'It had *everything* to do with me. The reason I came here tonight wasn't to find your secret lab. It was to bring the artefacts back and forget all about them. Actually, if you could just use that belt to do a number on me now, I'll be on my way.'

'Virgil, trust me, we can—'

'Tell me what happened to Floyd Burlock. Then we'll talk about trust.'

'Floyd was a terrible accident.' She turned herself with difficulty until she was facing him. 'I had been teasing him. Bringing him up to the graveyard, mere feet away from what his heart desired, then sending him home, dissatisfied. It was my own petty revenge for everything he put me through. Then, one afternoon, I napped too long. Jerome went out to mow the grass without telling me. I heard raised voices. They were wrestling under the cherry tree. I was invisible, of course. I went to break them up, forgetting I still held the knife.' She closed her eyes. 'Jerome was so upset, I had to wipe the entire event from his memory. But I couldn't bring myself to move Burlock, so I left him.'

'And when we found him?'

'Jerome would have been implicated, as would you. I couldn't have Burlock destroy two more people I cared about. So, I stood next to his body, wearing the belt. And convinced both you and those two young police officers that there was nothing there. The belt is incredibly persuasive. I waited until dark then buried the body.'

'I was right. You are crazy.'

'Virgil.'

'Wipe my memory too.' He took Goldie off and dropped her on the seat.

'Virgil, Jerome is dying.'

'What?'

'That trip to Leeds, to visit our son. It will be his last.'

Virgil slumped back into the chair. 'What's the matter with him?'

'Bowel Cancer. He has deteriorated so quickly these last few weeks that... it will be rapid now. God's little joke on me for messing with his mind.'

'Does he know about his diagnosis?'

'I don't expect you to condone the things I have done.'

'Does he know?'

Margaery pursed her lips; gave a blink and you'll miss it shake of her head.

Virgil stood up in disgust.

'Virgil, I will make it right. I'm going to come out of hiding. Back to village life. Be with Jerome for the time he has left. I owe it to him.'

'But what do you need me for? I won't be a part of your manipulation games.'

Margaery slipped off the belt. 'I want you to do to me what I have done to so many others; make Felicity Gardens a reality. Make it so I forget it all; Burlock, the crypt, I want it gone. All I want is my Jerome, to care for him, end it well.' She passed him a note. 'This is the location of Floyd's remains, I removed all of your DNA. Leaving only my own.' She handed over a second scrap of paper. 'Here is my confession. As soon as Jerome has passed on, you have my permission to hand it to the police. I'll do my time.' Finally, she held out the belt. 'Please, do it for Jerome's sake. He is a good man.'

Virgil stared into the belt's glittering skin until his eyes unfocused. A grandfather clock by the large round door chimed. She was still holding it out, expectantly.

Tentatively, he reached out and took the belt.

'I'll do it. But I have one more question.'

'Anything, dear.'

'What happened to Burlock's dog?'

Margaery dropped her head. When she raised it, her face told him this would be the truth.

'Cat's gotta eat,' she winced. 'The girls hated that mutt more than I hated Floyd.'

CHAPTER FORTY
CLOCKING OFF

There was quite the stir in Prestley when Margaery Yeboah came home. The Pastor's wife was in sound mind and claimed that her years of therapy had been transformative. She was looking forward to being involved in the community again. The Women's Institute held an impromptu welcome home party for her, where bashful old friends were delighted to find that Margaery bore no grudges about the shameful gossiping of yesteryear. Better still, she didn't seem to remember it at all.

The disappearance of Floyd Burlock spawned a few conspiracy theories, all of which could be heard if visiting his old haunt, the Royal Oak. As far as the general populace were concerned, Floyd's vanishing was completely overshadowed by Margaery's return. But the juxtaposition of the two events was not lost on some. An article appeared in the Prestley Press, written by an anonymous 'former postman' who refuted the idea that Mrs Yeboah had been entangled with Burlock. The police at the time, he claimed, were investigating the gardener himself for stalking. Other articles followed suit. Whether there was any truth in them, or whether they were Prestley's way of purging its collective conscience, didn't matter to Virgil. *Jerome has been hard done by, and if Marge's name can be cleared by the same folks who smeared it, so be it.*

A small part of him had resisted Margaery's solution right up until the last moment. The way she readily confessed to her life of subterfuge shocked him, even as he tried to understand her pain. The problem was, stood there with the crackling fire to his back and this woman who could erase the very foundations of his personality, Virgil couldn't see another way around it. He had taken the swinging belt from her reluctantly. As it left her hand, she had shrunk in the chair, a tired old woman.

The belt of truth was surprisingly intuitive; just as Goldie made him invincible, and the knife made him invisible, a touch of the belt gave him unfettered access to people's objective reality. Virgil thought it, and the belt delivered it. For Margaery, his command had been simple: 'She remembers nothing about her work. Floyd Burlock never existed.'

Jerome had been significantly harder, possibly because Virgil knew him better, but also because he was acutely aware that Marge had been doing this to him already. Regrettably, for the plan to work, both Yeboahs needed a soft-reset.

Now that Jerome and Marge were civilians, something had to be done about the crypt. Virgil's final act using Goldie was to cave in the tunnel that led to the Manse basement. When it was done, he returned both the shield strap and the knife to their respective sarcophagi and crawled out through the boards. After he had hammered the planks back into place, a pair of eyes shone out from between them, startling him like the first time.

'Zwingli, you dopey creature!' He went about undoing his handiwork while she licked herself. Was it possible for a cat to look guilty?

'I can't believe you ate Floyd's dog!'

~   ~   ~

Trent Pidgeon was released from custody pending further enquiries. The judge cited an administrative error as the reason for the case being dropped. Either way, the family were overjoyed and held a party to celebrate. Trent was dealing again in less than a fortnight. Virgil found out accidentally—Pidge pretended he didn't know.

~ ~ ~

Tony told Zelda about Trevor two months to the day after Virgil had caught him at the house. She was shocked at first and scared them by going quiet and retreating to her room, presumably to cry. When she emerged, a nerve-shredding hour later, her face was tear-free. She had prayed about it and believed in her heart that Tony had done the right thing. They would invite Trevor over for toffee apples and sausage rolls. Tony would ask the foster home about bringing Tabitha too. It was Bonfire night tomorrow after all.

When morning came on November 5th, Tony was more worked up than Zelda, and occupied himself cleaning the whole bungalow inside and out. He had to change his shirt before he left to pick up Tabitha, such were the sweat patches.

Virgil met Trevor at the bus stop and they walked up together. Trevor had bought a bouquet of lilies, which he held like one would hold a washed-up squid—unsure of which way up it went. He pin-balled from garden wall to kerbside, leaving a trail of petals in his wake. Even in the blustery air, he stank. Virgil fancied he could have set light to his breath. When Zelda opened the door, Trevor dropped the flowers on her lap then crumpled, touching her feet with the tip of his nose as he vomited out apologies. She pulled him up, whipping a tissue out of her apron for his snot-drivelled top lip.

'Thank you for being sorry,' she said, older and wiser and more powerful than Virgil had ever seen her. 'Come inside, there's tea in the pot.'

Maisie and Tabitha laughed like little drains, running from room to room with a toy shopping trolley and pram. Meanwhile, Virgil helped Tony and an ever more lucid Trevor set some rudimentary fireworks in the garden. The six of them huddled together in the crisp night air 'ooh-ing' and 'aah-ing' as the cheap rockets and fountains zinged light into the darkness. The Catherine wheel malfunctioned and went off with an almighty bang which set the girls off crying, quickly ending the show.

Tony drove Trevor and Tabitha home, while Virgil helped get Maisie to bed. When his little sister was snoring, he knocked on Zelda's bedroom door.

'Come in.'

'You must be shattered, Mum.'

'I never thought I could see that man again,' Zelda said into the mirror, taking off her earrings and laying them in the drawer.

'How was it?' He bit his lip, leaning against the wardrobe.

'Difficult. But it didn't feel wrong.' Zelda frowned, 'I suppose it was cathartic, in a way.'

'Do you think we'll have them over here again?'

'Would Maisie ever speak to us again if we didn't?'

'Huh. They did play nicely. Can I get you anything before I go?'

'I'm all set, darling. Don't stay up too late.'

'Night, Mum.'

'Goodnight, Virgil.'

'Mum?'

'Yes?'

'Is Dad coming home?'

'Would you like him to?'

'Would *you*?'

Zelda smiled.

~ ~ ~

Virgil had only been to one funeral: Gramps'. His dad had worn a blue suit. The flowers had been white and had set off Aunt Julie's allergies. That was about all he could remember.

The Saxo victims were far more memorable. Held at Saint Anne's in Fleddley on consecutive days, each funeral packed the tiny church out and turned Main Street into one long traffic jam. Virgil attended all three. Sitting at the back, wallowing in the crummy songs and tributes which sounded nothing like the knuckle-draggers he had encountered. While Kade's open casket was being swamped by wailing high-heels, his brother, Damian, sat bolt-upright on the front row. He was twitchy and kept looking back at Virgil, snapping away as soon as their eyes met. There was a fair amount of overlap between the guest lists and Virgil feared being recognised, the papers hadn't named him, but news travelled fast in these parts. Remarkably, the family and friends of Kade Wurzel and Patrick Jones filed past in their salt-eyed droves and not a word was said. The third time around, Virgil was not so lucky as an incandescent uncle fell upon him as his nephew's coffin sailed past.

'I know you. You're the one who got in their car! You're the one who got our boys killed. HE'S THE ONE!

HE'S THE—' Virgil let the jowly old dog rage at him for a while. He didn't even wipe the spit from his face. *He's right.* Only when Benjamin Gill's uncle grabbed him around the collar did Virgil reach for the belt. Touching it with one finger, he convinced the man that he was greeting an old friend. He was crushed in a bear-hug and kissed wetly, then released.

Virgil spent the rest of November at the Manse, stroking cats and eating banana bread while he poured out his heart to the Yeboahs. They were great listeners and good company, and Virgil felt bad every time he left, wiping their entire interaction clean of Crypt-talk.

Jerome died on the 10th of December. The thanksgiving service was so packed, it spilled out into the graveyard and ended with African dancing and songs in the snow. When he got home, Virgil stared at Margaery's confession for a long time. It was at this strange and ironic moment that Floyd Burlock's own words spoke to him from the stolen diary:

'It's hard to feel guilty for something you don't remember doing.'

Marge had no recollection of any of her crimes. It wasn't like she was living it up, cackling to herself about the fact she had got away with it all. After all those years she had spent in self-imposed solitude, it didn't seem fair to have her banged up again. She would die in prison not even knowing why. Hoping he was doing the right thing, Virgil burned the confession and the map to Floyd's body. Afterwards, he went out into the garden and was sick.

He told himself that his crime-fighting days were over. He had been proven unfit for the task. Those three lads would never park in a disabled bay again. *They'll never park anywhere again.* He would leave the Ram behind, go back to being a weed. His dad's mantra: head down, keep walking. *Just Virgil McAllister. Just me.*

The belt would go back.

CHAPTER FORTY-ONE
NOTHING PERSONAL

'How've you been, Virge? Oh, happy new year by the way.'

'Happy new year, Pidge. Yeah, I'm feeling better. Been helping Dad retile that patch of roof that blew off.'

'Cool, cool. Listen, I know it might be too soon, but I've fixed the drone's night vision and I wondered if you wanted to...'

'I'd love to. It's about time the Ram saw action again.'

'Really?'

'Yeah, why not?'

'I was worried you'd packed it all in.'

'Came close to it. I even went back down to the crypt on Christmas Eve and stood there with the lid open and the belt in my hand. But...'

'But what?'

'I dunno, I just felt like... like Prestley still needed us. And let's face it, with Goldie and that knife out of the picture, I'm less likely to, you know...'

'Kill anyone.'

'You didn't need to say it.'

'I did. You know my take: what happened wasn't your fault. You just wanted closure.'

'I wanted revenge. And I got it.'

After a long pause, Virgil broke the silence. 'Look, Pidge, I am still in. I just think we need stricter rules.'

'Such as?'

'It's never allowed to be personal. That was Marge's downfall, and it will be ours if we're not honest with ourselves. You getting Trent out of the nick... me and the Saxo lads... Daniel Dauber.'

'Gosh, why do you have to be such a deep thinker? You're right, of course. Nothing personal. We roam, we step in, we leave things better than when we got there. Deal?'

'Deal. Right, I'm nearly home.'

'Laters, Krav Maggot.'

'See you, Daniel Dorker.'

Virgil closed his phone case and pocketed the earbuds. The bus was crawling into Mickleover, two more stops. He hadn't brought the Ram mask—he wouldn't need it. Running his fingers over his crown, he prodded the afro that was growing back. The belt sat snugly over his midriff. It was warm, a part of him. It didn't matter now whether his mask was nylon or not; he never got to fighting these days.

As he had long suspected, even when Goldie had him in her grip, there were some problems a pair of fists couldn't solve. With the right word, a brush of the belt, Virgil administered violence-free justice. He had even stopped thinking of himself as a vigilante. *I'm a peacemaker now.*

The path up to Trevor Lee's door was clear of vines, he and his dad had seen to that a few weeks back—part of the pact. The road to recovery. Truth was, dear old Trevs wasn't recovering. Sure, he attended AA with legalistic regularity, but he drank even more religiously. Even Tony admitted he couldn't see it happening unless Trevor's attitude changed. *But what if we could change his attitude for him?*

Virgil steadied himself, keeping one hand firmly around the belt. One thought would do it. One thought:

'Remember, Trev, you can't stand alcohol.'

He reached up a trembling hand and knocked twice.

ACKNOWLEDGEMENTS

Firstly, I would like to thank you, dear reader, for buying this book. As a beginner with a lot to learn, your support is a big deal. To everyone who has encouraged me in my writing, especially those friends who talked to me about my characters, thank you.

To my focus readers: Terry, Luke and Deb. Thank you for giving up your time to vet Virgil.

To my editor, Laura Wilkinson, your attention to detail and sublime wordsmithery saved me from many a plot hole.

To Walt, the King of Formatting, your design skills are formidable, I owe you big time.

To Mum, thank you for your advice both medical and sociological and for the hours you spent in Virgil's world.

Lastly, I would like to thank my beautiful wife, Joh, who puts up with me rolling into bed after writing until 2AM. Your support of my work is a great blessing.

At the time of writing I am a self-published author. If you enjoyed this book, and have a moment, please leave a review on Amazon. Thank you!

Printed in Poland
by Amazon Fulfillment
Poland Sp. z o.o., Wrocław

64668289R00186